BACK TO PAUL REVERE!

BACK TO PAUL REVERE!

Beatrice Gormley

AN
APPLE
PAPERBACK

SCHOLASTIC INC.
New York Toronto London Auckland Sydney

ISBN 0-590-46227-X

12 11 10 9 8 7 6 5 4 3 2 1   4 5 6 7 8 9/9

Printed in the U.S.A.   40

First Scholastic printing, November 1994

Contents

BACK TO PAUL REVERE!

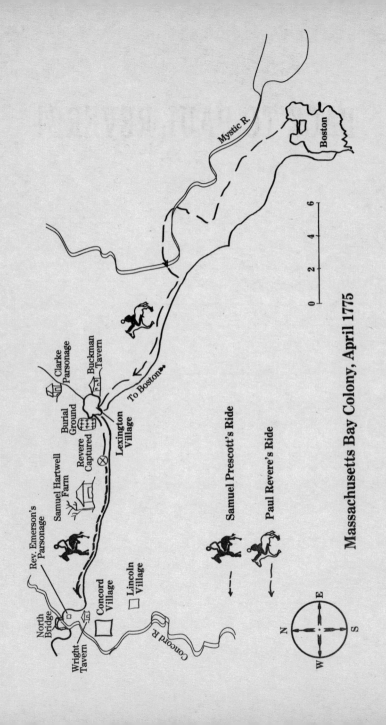

Massachusetts Bay Colony, April 1775

1.
The Most Exciting Moment

Emily Cowen, age ten, bounded down the hall toward her older brother's room. Her softball glove swung from one hand. "Matt!" She pushed the door open. "Mom wants us to take the TASC back to Grandpa Frank *this afternoon.*"

Matt and his friend Jonathan Schultz, both twelve, were stretched out on the floor with a skateboard catalog. At Emily's announcement, Jonathan shook a lock of dark hair out of his eyes and pushed himself up on his long, skinny arms. "What? Why?"

"Mom dropped by to see Grandpa Frank before she picked me up from softball," said Emily. "She said he was worried that we might get hurt fooling around with the TASC. Mom thought he meant get an electrical shock, or something."

Matt didn't look nearly as upset as Jonathan. In fact, Emily noticed, her brother didn't even seem that surprised. He was studying the skate-

1

board catalog very intently, as if he didn't want to look Emily or Jonathan in the eye.

"Matt!" Emily punched her softball glove to make a double exclamation. "What did you tell Grandpa Frank?"

"Well — when I saw him a couple of days ago, he said he noticed the TASC wasn't back in his workshop yet. So I told him we'd bring it back this weekend." Matt put on his mature-older-brother expression. "Listen, we shouldn't even think of using it again. Don't you guys understand that? I mean, yeah, at first I thought we'd have to give it another try. But think for a minute about what almost happened on the trip to the *Titanic*!"

"But that's only because we didn't plan it out the way we should have," argued Jonathan. "We could definitely do better, next trip." He unfolded himself from the floor and stepped over to the object in a corner of the room, hidden by a gray barbecue grill cover. He gripped the cover with his long fingers, as if Matt were going to grab the TASC from him.

"Right." Emily marched across the room to stand beside Jonathan. "For one thing, next time we should stick together instead of going off different ways. Then we won't have to run around hunting for each other when the ship's sinking or whatever."

"Oh, right — like it's as simple as that," said Matt. But he followed them to the corner. With Matt and Emily watching, Jonathan pulled the cover off the TASC, as though he were unveiling a priceless statue.

Actually, thought Emily, anyone who hadn't seen the TASC in action would laugh at the way it looked. Her great-grandfather's invention was a mishmash of instruments and appliances and other equipment, fastened on the three shelves of a metal cart. Wires and cables looped from the blender on the bottom shelf to the digital clocks and batteries on the middle shelf to the opaque projector on the top.

TASC stood for Time and Space Connector. A way to travel in time. It worked. *How* it worked, Emily had no idea. Neither did Matt, or anyone else except its inventor, their great-grandfather. And of course Jonathan, who was some kind of science genius.

Naturally Grandpa Frank wanted them to give back his junky looking contraption, fastened together with bolts and brackets and electrical tape. Of course he was afraid they were going to use it again. Who wouldn't? Emily couldn't believe Matt wanted to give it up.

Beside Emily, Matt was staring at the TASC, his gray-blue eyes glazed. He wiggled his shoulders, as if he felt some kind of spell closing in on him. "Well . . . maybe we could keep it one more day. Think this thing over. But we need a reason why we can't take it back today."

"Because it's raining," suggested Jonathan.

Emily glanced out the window at the spring drizzle dripping from the blossoming pear tree. "No good. I had softball practice anyway."

"I've got it." Matt looked pleased with himself. "We have to go to the library this afternoon. We all have reports due on Monday."

"Very important reports." Emily giggled, partly because Matt was coming around to her point of view. "History reports."

Jonathan grinned. "Yeah, now I remember that assignment. Something like, 'If you could visit any moment in history, which one would you choose? Explain.' "

"The most exciting moment," added Emily.

Matt looked away from the TASC. He pushed his hands into his pockets, the way he did when something was bothering him. "I don't know. I sort of wanted to wait a while, after . . ."

Emily knew what her brother meant: After their first trip with the Time and Space Connector. After what had happened on the *Titanic*.

"Yeah, but this is our only chance." Jonathan traced one of the cables on the TASC with his long, skinny fingers. "Once Mr. Kenny gets this back, he'll never let us have it again. He might even take it apart."

4

Matt frowned at his sneakers, as if an argument was going on inside his head. Then his forehead smoothed out, and his hands popped out of his pockets. "Okay." He started walking back and forth. "So we've only got today and tonight to use the TASC one more time. So we should make good use of it. We should go to the most exciting moment in history, which is — "

" — the Wright brothers' flight at Kittyhawk!" Jonathan's thin, dark face lit up.

" — the American Revolution!" exclaimed Emily. A vision flashed through her mind: a horse and rider thundering down a moonlit road.

Matt frowned from his friend to his sister. "*As I was saying,* which is the Battle of Gettysburg, in the Civil War."

"Boo, hiss." Jonathan made a thumbs-down sign.

Emily took a breath to argue with Matt and Jonathan, but just then the front doorbell rang. "That must be the marketing guy who was coming to talk to Dad," said Matt. "Dad told me to let him in, in case he was on the phone."

Emily and Jonathan followed Matt into the hall and watched from the top of the stairs as he opened the door. The man in the doorway, wearing a raincoat and carrying a briefcase, raised his eyebrows at Matt. "Hallo! George Kingsley to see Daniel Cowen — if I have the proper address."

"Yeah, come on in," said Matt. "Dad must be on the phone." He nodded down a second flight of stairs to the door of their father's office. "Want to come up and sit in the living room for a minute?" He took the man's raincoat and hung it in the hall closet while Mr. Kingsley climbed the stairs.

"Hello." Emily gave Mr. Kingsley a smile. An idea struck her, and she leaned forward on the railing. "You know, we were just having this argument. Maybe you could help us decide — "

"Emily." For some reason, Matt was looking up the stairs at her with a pained expression. "Mr. Kingsley isn't going to go for *any* of our ideas, because — "

"Try me," said Mr. Kingsley brightly. "Always glad to be of service."

Matt started to talk again, but Emily interrupted. "We're trying to decide what was the most exciting moment in history. Wouldn't you say it was the American Revolution?"

Mr. Kingsley gave a surprised laugh, as if she'd made a joke. Matt said, *"Emily,"* again. Jonathan rolled his eyes.

Emily felt her face get warm, but she still didn't understand what her mistake was until Mr. Kingsley opened his mouth again. "The so-called American Revolution? That ungrateful, disloyal gang of peasants and rabble, committing treason against the British Empire? What

6

an idea, my dear. What *do* they teach you Yanks in school? Surely there's nothing so exciting about a lot of Colonials trying to get out of paying taxes."

Now Emily recognized Mr. Kingsley's clipped accent. He was British. She would have felt silly, if she hadn't been angry instead. "The taxes weren't fair," she snapped, "because we didn't have a chance to vote on them."

Matt, not usually one to argue with adults, spoke up. "Anyway, Mr. Kingsley, you have to admit, the Revolution was about a lot more than taxes."

"I'll admit that's the way the propaganda goes." Mr. Kingsley smiled. His teeth were yellowish, and his eyes almost disappeared in the wrinkled folds of his eyelids. "Oh, the Colonies were willing enough to be protected from the French and Indians by His Majesty's troops. But they weren't willing to pay the bill."

"*We* fought in the French and Indian Wars." Jonathan drew himself up to his full skinny height. "It wasn't just British troops protecting the Colonies."

"Besides," said Emily, "the British Parliament had no right to make laws for us without giving us any say. *That* was the main thing. The British were trying to take away our freedom!"

Mr. Kingsley laughed and backed down a step, pretending to be afraid. "What a little firebrand you are. It must go with your red hair." His glance shifted down the stairs, where Mr. Cowen had appeared. "Ah, Dan."

"Sorry to keep you waiting, George." Mr. Cowen, a stocky man with wavy, sandy hair like Matt's, hurried up the two flights of stairs. He shook hands with Mr. Kingsley. "Come on down to my office. We'll go over those sales figures before we head out for lunch." He turned to the kids. "You're taking that invention thing back to Grandpa Frank, right?"

Emily, still glaring at the British visitor, couldn't answer. But Matt said smoothly, "Yeah, we can do that tomorrow. We have to go to the library this afternoon. We all have history reports due."

With a nod as if he was already thinking about business again, Mr. Cowen ushered Mr. Kingsley down the stairs. "A pleasure chatting with you kids," said the Britisher over his shoulder.

As the door of Mr. Cowen's office closed behind the two men, Emily muttered, "A *dis*pleasure, for me."

"Yeah, he didn't have to be such a jerk." Matt rattled the iron railing on the stairs.

"Some adults are like that." Jonathan's eyes were narrowed. "They're adults and we're kids, so naturally they must know more. What would Mr. Kingsley know about the American Revolution?"

"Nothing," answered Emily. "He's only putting it down because he's British, and they lost."

Arguing seemed to have made the kids hungry, and they wandered out to the kitchen for a snack. Opening the refrigerator, Matt stared into its depths. "But look at it another way: What do *I* know about the American Revolution? All I know is what I've been taught. Maybe I want to think the Colonists were all heroes because I'm American, and we won."

"What're you talking about, man?" Jonathan's normally calm voice cracked a bit. "The British came over here and tried to tell the American Colonists how to run their lives. We said no way, we'd rather fight. We won. End of story." But he was frowning, as if he weren't quite that sure.

"Yeah, Matt," Emily told her brother. "Cut it out. You sound like Mr. Kingsley."

Emily had calmed down a bit, but now she was getting mad all over again. Energy sizzled up and down her arms and legs, and she wanted to do something with it. Like stepping toward the plate with her baseball bat and hitting a ball, *thunk*. Instead, she grabbed an apple from the fruit bowl and chomped into it. She turned away from Matt, fixing her gaze on the refrigerator.

The Cowens' refrigerator door was covered with notes on yellow tags, with Emily's softball schedule, with snapshots of friends and relatives. And with postcards, like the one Dad had sent last month from a business trip to Massachusetts. The picture showed a graveyard with headstones, and their father had made a joke on the card about the nice rest he'd had there.

Jonathan lifted a bag of pretzels from the top of the refrigerator and opened it expertly, without ripping the bag. "You know, there's one way to find out for sure."

"To find out — ?" Matt helped himself to pretzels. Then he stared from Jonathan to Emily, an intense light in his gray-blue eyes. "Hey — I just decided what I'm going to do my history report on."

Jonathan smiled. "On that gang of peasants and rabble acting disloyal to the British Empire, right?"

"Yes!" Emily laughed out loud. They'd just agreed on where to go with the Time and Space Connector — and Emily had won.

A short while later, Matt and Emily and Jonathan trotted up the steps of the public library. "The question is," said Matt, "what exact date do we want to go to? The Revolution took years. We don't want to be away much longer than we were on the *Titanic,* right?"

"Nobody will know how long we're gone," Jonathan pointed out. "The TASC brings you back to the present on the exact second after you leave. But yeah, I guess we'd run into problems if we stayed there more than a day or so."

Emily pressed forward through the library turnstile, leaving Matt and Jonathan discussing whether they could stay at an inn in 1775 without actually paying 1775 money. She'd spotted a shelf against the wall labeled OVERSIZE — HISTORY. The oversize books were the ones with the best pictures. And Matt and Jonathan might have forgotten it, but they needed a picture for the TASC.

When the three of them traveled to the *Titanic,* to 1912, they'd put a photo of the ship's boat deck in the projector part of the Time and Space Connector. The invention had projected the picture onto Matt's bedroom wall, blown up to life size. Then Emily and Matt and Jonathan had stood in front of the projector to fit into the picture. Then Jonathan had pressed the TRANSPORT button . . .

Emily read the titles on the spines of the books. *Civil War Art. An American Album. A Pictorial History of the American Revolution —* that last one sounded promising.

Emily lifted the heavy coffee-table book from the shelf and flipped a few pages. There was a painting of Paul Revere in his shirtsleeves, one hand on a silver teapot. A half-smile curved the corners of his mouth.

Paul Revere, thought Emily, he's the one. Only not this scene.

She turned another page. There it was. She'd seen this picture before, the rider with the three-cornered hat shouting up at the windows of a house, the horse with all four legs gathered under him in a gallop, the moon lighting up the faces of horse and rider and the startled people peering from the windows. Emily's heart beat faster, and her throat tightened.

This picture showed the way Emily thought of the American Revolution. It was exciting, it was dangerous. It was *heroic*. It made her proud. And that was why Emily had gotten so angry at Mr. Kingsley. He had tried to take that pride away from her.

"Here it is!" Emily announced to Matt and Jonathan. She lugged *A Pictorial History* into the aisle of regular-sized history books, where the boys were browsing. "I've got the picture."

Matt lifted the book from Emily's hands. "Cool! The midnight ride of Paul Revere. The beginning of the Revolution, that's exactly what — " He stopped, frowning thoughtfully.

Jonathan peered over Matt's shoulder. "Uh-oh." He pushed his dark hair out of his eyes, as if he hadn't seen the picture clearly. "What was I thinking? I got so mad at Mr. King George or whatever his name is, I lost it."

"What do you mean?" demanded Emily. "What's wrong?"

"He means we can't use this picture," said Matt slowly. "And besides that, the real bummer is . . . we can't go back to the American Revolution at all. Because we have to have a *photograph* for the TASC."

"We can't go — ? But I've got the picture!" exclaimed Emily. "Here it is, Paul Revere's . . . Oh." She felt as if a door had slammed in her face. "You mean, this picture is just how someone *imagined* Paul Revere's ride. A painting."

Jonathan nodded, looking sorry. "Obviously they weren't standing there with an easel set up, when Paul Revere came riding through. But even if they had been, it still wouldn't be a photograph. It wouldn't be a precise image of reality."

Matt blew out his breath with a loud noise, like a horse. "Bummer!" he said again. He turned another page of Emily's book, to a painting of a wooden bridge over a stream. Soldiers in scarlet coats stood on one side, men in three-cornered hats and everyday clothes on the other. Blue musket smoke floated in between them. " 'The Battle of Concord,' " Matt read out loud. " 'The shot heard 'round the world.' "

"I can't believe it!" Emily burst out. Just as

13

she was rushing headlong toward this adventure, as if she herself were galloping on horseback — it had vanished. She looked pleadingly from Matt to Jonathan. "There has to be some way."

Jonathan shrugged glumly. "The TASC needs a real picture. A scene in 1775, just the way it was then."

Matt was reading to himself again. After a few moments, he sighed. "You know, it really is too bad, because this would be the perfect trip. We could land in Lexington just before midnight, in time to see Paul Revere come riding in. And then at dawn there was a battle in Lexington, and later that morning there was a battle in Concord. All within a few miles."

"Too bad. But you can't get around reality." Jonathan shrugged again. "We can't time-travel to anywhere before the camera was invented. Of course," he went on in a more cheerful voice, "the camera was invented way before the Wright brothers' flight at Kittyhawk."

Matt brightened. "Even before the Battle of Gettysburg."

Emily didn't say anything. I don't want to go anywhere except the Revolution, she thought.

It seemed that their discussion of where to go with the TASC was back to square one. When the three kids left the library, Matt was carrying a book titled *The War Between the States,* and Jonathan had *Triumph at Kittyhawk.*

As for Emily, behind Matt and Jonathan on the sidewalk, she was lugging *A Pictorial History of the American Revolution.* Watching the drizzle collect on the book's plastic cover, she knew she was being stubborn and unreasonable. But she refused to believe that the TASC couldn't *somehow* take them to 1775. What good was a time machine that only worked within the last 150 years?

What good was a time machine that couldn't take you to the most exciting moment in history?

2.
Destination: 1775

When they got home, Mr. Kingsley's blue rented car was still in front of the house, but Mr. Cowen's car was gone from the driveway. "I guess they went out to lunch," remarked Matt. "Speaking of lunch . . ." He led Emily and Jonathan into the kitchen, where they set their books on the table and pulled out bread and cold cuts and other sandwich fixings.

A few minutes later Matt and Jonathan were sitting at the kitchen table with their sandwiches. Emily put her plate down, then went back to the refrigerator for pickles. As she closed the refrigerator door, something on the outside caught her eye.

It was the postcard that Dad had sent them last month. From somewhere in Massachusetts. A picture — a *photograph* — of an old graveyard.

A shiver of hope went through Emily as she stared at the headstones in the picture. She yanked the postcard off the refrigerator, turned it over, and read the printing in the upper left corner.

OLD BURYING GROUND
LEXINGTON, MASSACHUSETTS

"Yow!" she screamed.

Matt's and Jonathan's heads jerked up from their sandwiches. Matt shoved his chair back. "Did you pinch your finger?"

"No, no, no." Emily shook the postcard at them. "A *photograph*. Of a place in Lexington, a place that was there in 1775. And even a spot where we could fit in." She pointed to a stretch of grass between headstones.

"Nice try, Em," said Matt. He went back to the table and picked up his sandwich. "Sure, it's a photograph. But obviously it wasn't taken in 1775."

"So what?" asked Emily. *"Obviously* that photo of the *Titanic* we used wasn't taken the day the ship sank."

"Yeah, but there's a little difference between two days and two centuries," said Jonathan. "That graveyard could have looked entirely different then."

"No, it couldn't," said Emily. "Read the dates on the gravestones."

Jonathan took the postcard from Emily and

17

studied the picture of the Old Burying Ground. "Hm." He pointed to the large headstone on the left.

"HERE LYES BURIED
THE BODY OF
MR. JONATHAN SIMONDS
WHO DEPARTED THIS LIFE
FEBRY 22D, 1747,
AGED 56 YEARS."

Emily put her forefinger on the large headstone on the right. "And this one says Mr. Hezekiah Smith departed this life in *1760*."

Matt leaned toward the postcard, chewing. "So what you're saying is, that empty space in between the headstones has been there at least from 1760 to the time the picture was taken." He shifted his sandwich to the other hand and tapped the grassy stretch in the picture. "So this spot in the graveyard must have looked like this in 1775."

"Watch it!" Jonathan jerked the postcard away. "You just got mustard on the only picture we have to use in the TASC, man." He wiped the picture gently with the bottom of his T-shirt.

Emily laughed triumphantly. "Yes! We *can* use this picture in the TASC!"

"Hold on — I don't know," said Jonathan. "I didn't mean I'm sure we can use it. I have to

18

think about this." He sat down again, propping the postcard against the napkin holder to study while he munched his way through his sandwich.

Matt and Emily sat down to eat their sandwiches, too. Matt opened Emily's library book, *A Pictorial History of the American Revolution.* "If this worked," he said with his mouth full, "it would be perfect. See, the Old Burying Ground in Lexington is right near the village common. Not that far from the parsonage, which is where Paul Revere was heading on the night of April eighteenth, to warn John Hancock and Sam Adams."

"April eighteenth?" Jonathan washed down his last bite of sandwich with milk. "I hate to tell you this, but I think we already missed our chance to see Paul Revere's ride and so on. Remember, when we went to the *Titanic,* it was the same month and day here that it was there?"

Matt stared at his friend and groaned. "And today is April twenty-second."

Emily groaned, too. "You mean we'd have to wait until *next year?*" She couldn't believe it, just after she'd found the picture. "Jonathan. You could fiddle around with the TASC and make it work for us today, couldn't you? I'm sure you could. You're a genius."

Jonathan looked flattered, but he shook his head. "I'm not so sure. The way the TASC operates, resonance is the key. That's how the crystal functions to coordinate the vibrations from two different spots in the space-time matrix."

Emily exchanged a glance with her brother. She could see that Matt didn't know what Jonathan was talking about, either. All they knew was that it had something to do with the rose quartz fastened over the lens of the projector on the TASC.

Sitting up straight, Matt slapped his hands on the table. "Whatever. Maybe it won't work, but either we're going to try, or we aren't. I think we should work as hard as we can to reset the TASC and make costumes and plan the trip, until we run out of time tonight. Then we can decide whether to go or not."

Jonathan pushed back his chair. "Cool. I'd better get to work on the TASC. Just for starters, the location finder is going to need a lot of adjusting."

Matt went to the garage to get the Cowens' seldom-used toolbox for Jonathan. Then they all returned to Matt's room. Jonathan began to tinker with their great-grandfather's invention, while Emily and Matt sat on the floor and studied the pictures in her library book.

"It's a good thing you brought this book home, after all," remarked Matt. "These pictures are excellent for planning our costumes."

At first they thought they'd have to find a long

Colonial-style dress for Emily. Then Emily had the bright idea of dressing like a boy, which would be much more comfortable. "I'll tie my hair back, the way boys did then." Emily pushed her curly red hair to the nape of her neck with both hands. "Hey — I'm Ethan!"

But that idea made them realize that Matt and Jonathan were going to have to wear wigs, so their hair would look normal for 1775. "Geeky," grumbled Jonathan, glancing up from the section of the TASC that he was unbolting.

"We're lucky that some Colonial boys *did* wear wigs," retorted Matt. "So our wigs don't have to look like real hair."

Matt and Emily started searching the house for costume items. In their mother's dresser Emily discovered a vampire-lady wig, left over from Halloween.

"That'll work for Jonathan," said Matt. "But I think we're going to have to buy one for me. Let's see how much money we have."

Bartley's Bargains, a store only a few blocks away, did have a light brown wig for Matt. The store also had a photocopy machine, and Matt had brought the library book along to make a copy of a map.

"Is there anything else we have to buy while we're here?" asked Matt, dropping coins in the copy machine.

Emily gazed regretfully at the shiny belt

buckles on one of the racks. Buckles would have been a nice Colonial touch on their shoes, but the kids had already spent most of their money on the wig. "I think all we really need for clothes is a white shirt and a pair of knee pants apiece. We can cut off old jeans."

"No, we can't." Matt pushed the PRINT button. "No zippers. The Colonists didn't have zippers."

"You say no zippers, and you're making a Xerox copy to take?" Emily raised an eyebrow at him. "The Colonists sure didn't have ye olde Xerox machine!"

"Yeah, but they won't *know* this is a Xerox." Matt held up a map of the Battle Road between Lexington and Concord. "See, if you're used to buttons and strings, and you see a zipper, it looks really weird. But if you've never heard of photocopies, and you see this" — he waved the map — "you'd just think someone drew it."

Emily gazed at the map. "Which way does Paul Revere come?"

Matt put a finger on one side of the paper. "This road. Past the village common — that triangle — and up this other road to the parsonage. Then when he leaves the parsonage, he'll ride down this road toward Concord."

"And that's the graveyard?" Emily pointed to a little plot with crosses. "So after we land, all we have to do is walk down the road a little way — and we'll see Paul Revere ride in." She caught her breath at the thought.

When Emily and Matt got home from the store, Jonathan was kneeling on the floor of Matt's room, next to the TASC cart. "What are you doing?" exclaimed Emily. There was almost nothing on the shelves of the cart. The parts of the Time and Space Connector were spread out over the carpet like items in a garage sale.

Matt pushed his hands into his pockets, looking uneasy. "How's it going, Schultz?"

Jonathan, poring over the field of junk, didn't seem to hear. He was humming tunelessly, deep in thought. Emily whispered to her brother, "How's he going to get it back together in time? It's almost five o'clock."

"Better leave him alone," Matt whispered back. "We'll go ahead and do the costumes."

As Emily and Matt found pieces for their costumes, they laid them out on Matt's bed. In Mrs. Cowen's closet they discovered two white shirts, about the right size for Jonathan and Matt, with full sleeves. Emily could wear a white blouse of her own, as well as her vest. Each of the kids had a pair of leather shoes without laces and a leather belt. Mr. Cowen's dresser provided knee socks for Matt and Jonathan.

Emily had to admit that Matt had thought of a good way to avoid zippers: sweatpants. They took three old pairs and cut them off at the knees.

"We have to hem the legs and put drawstrings in them," said Matt, "but I guess we can do that after dinner." Stepping over to Jonathan, he waved a hand in front of his friend's glazed eyes. "Hey, Schultz. My father's ordering Chinese takeout. What do you want? And you'd better go home before dinner and get your shoes, and your overnight stuff."

After dinner, Mr. and Mrs. Cowen left for the movies. Emily and Matt and Jonathan hurried back to Matt's room. It made Emily nervous to look at the TASC, which was still half on the floor. "Do you think it's going to take a long time to get it back together?" she asked Jonathan.

"Don't know," he said. "I'm going nuts, just changing the geographical coordinates." He picked up an object that looked like the base of a telephone and pried the casing up with a screwdriver. "This baby wasn't built to go any-where except the *Titanic*."

Emily looked at her brother. Matt seemed worried, too. But he only wiggled his hands in his pockets and said, "Well, I guess adjusting a time machine isn't exactly changing a bicycle tire. Anyway, we still have a lot to do, ourselves."

It did take a lot longer than Emily expected for her and Matt to hem the three cutoff sweatpants and thread a drawstring through the bottom of each leg. Matt knew how to do this from making a gym bag in home ec, but all the hems had to be sewn by hand.

After the costumes were complete and waiting for them on Matt's plaid bedspread, they discussed what else they should take. "Something to eat," suggested Emily. "But it has to fit into the sweatpants pockets."

"And it has to be something normal for the Massachusetts Bay Colony in 1775," said Matt.

Raisins seemed like the best idea, except that they were sticky and likely to pick up pocket fluff. Plastic sandwich bags were out, of course. Luckily Matt thought of some handkerchiefs with his initials that he'd gotten as an unwanted Christmas present.

"Hey, Schultz." Matt spoke over his shoulder, tucking a handkerchief full of raisins into a pocket of each of the costumes on his bed. "Is the TASC ready to roll, or what? It's after eleven — my parents are going to be back pretty soon."

Stretching his arms and blinking as if he were coming out of a trance, Jonathan backed away from the Time and Space Connector. His gaze fell on the costumes, and he stuck his hand into a pocket of his knee pants on the bed. He frowned.

"What's wrong?" asked Emily.

"These pockets aren't deep enough." Jonathan fetched the TASC control from the TASC cart and pushed it into the pocket. "See how the control sticks out? What if it *fell* out? And a horse stepped on it?"

Chills ran down Emily's back. She stared at the TASC control, a gadget like the remote control for a TV. Once they were in 1775, that little rectangle with buttons would be their lifeline to return to the present. "We don't have time to make knee breeches out of another pair of pants."

"Besides," said Matt to Jonathan, "other pants have zippers. We can't wear zippers. What you need is some kind of pouch to tie to your belt."

"Pouch — Dad's aftershave!" exclaimed Emily. She ran out of the room. Fortunately her father had kept the brown leather pouch that his tall bottle of fancy aftershave lotion had come in.

By the time Emily returned with the pouch, Jonathan had placed the postcard from Lexington in the projector part of the TASC and turned it on. A field with rows of headstones overlay the posters on the wall behind Matt's bed. The scene was tinted pink, from the crystal fastened over the projector lens.

Jonathan narrowed his eyes at the graveyard scene. "I'm just not sure how this picture is going to affect the transport process. There's a *small* chance that some of our molecules won't end up in the year the clock" — he waved a hand at one of the digital clocks on the middle shelf of the cart — "is set for. Some of them might just naturally gravitate to the year the photograph was taken."

Emily stared at him. *"What?"*

Matt made a choked noise before he could get words out. "You're kidding. We spend all this time making the costumes, and — "

" — and we use up all our money on Matt's wig," put in Emily.

"And now you tell us," Matt went on, "if we try to use the TASC, some part of me that I just might need, like a kneecap or a liver, is going to end up in 1986?"

"Probably not," said Jonathan, as if they were getting upset over nothing. "But I thought I should mention it."

"Whatever." Emily couldn't stand to wait one moment longer, no matter what might go wrong. She grabbed her costume. "You two can sit around *mentioning* if you want, but I'm getting dressed."

A short while later Emily returned from her room in her white shirt, vest, knee pants, white kneesocks, and moccasins. "Aren't you guys ready yet? Mom and Dad will be back any minute." She helped Jonathan settle the vampire-lady wig on his head, and they tied each other's hair back with black ribbon.

Then the kids took down the posters and pushed Matt's bed out of the way. Jonathan stuck three lengths of tape on the carpet between the projector and the wall, so they'd stand in exactly the right spots.

Taking her place on the tape, facing the projector, Emily glanced over her shoulder at the picture on the wall. It looked a lot different than it had on the postcard. "Why did they used to put pictures of *skulls* on gravestones?" she asked.

"Yeah, and how did we end up going to a graveyard at midnight?" Giving a nervous laugh, Matt stepped into place beside her. "I'm glad it's April, instead of Halloween."

Jonathan stretched his arms over his head and made claws with his hands to cast a ghoulish shadow on the graveyard scene. But his laugh sounded just as nervous as Matt's.

"Hurry!" urged Emily. She had just heard a car engine in the driveway. "Mom and Dad are home."

"Let's *do* it," said Matt.

Jonathan held out the TASC control. "Okay. Don't move. Transport."

For a moment nothing happened.

"Why didn't we shut my door?" muttered Matt.

"Don't move," said Jonathan, barely moving his own lips.

Matt swallowed so hard that Emily heard it. He said hoarsely, "The tingling's starting."

Emily felt it, too. It was very hard to hold still. But the tingling meant they were on their way to another time and place.

And then Emily felt herself picked up and turned upside down and flung this way and that, like that time in the surf at Montauk. Except she wasn't even in water — she was nowhere.

Through her panic Emily thought, This is worse than last time. What does that mean?

Maybe it meant what Jonathan had *mentioned:* Some of their molecules might be ending up in the wrong year.

3.
The End of Mr. Revere's Ride

This wasn't Matt's first journey through time and space. But I'll never get used to it, he thought.

How could you get used to being turned into a stream of electrons or whatever (Jonathan had tried to explain it to him once), arcing between two points in the space-time matrix? You couldn't see or hear or feel anything in the normal way. It was more like being a ghost than Matt liked to think about.

And this time there was some kind of weird turbulence, too. Did that mean something had gone wrong?

"Unh!" Matt's feet met the ground with a jolt. But he didn't mind the jolt, he was so thankful to feel his feet again. His eyes could just barely make out the shapes of Emily and Jonathan beside him.

Stumbling, Matt bumped into his friend. Jonathan lurched away and bumped into something else. "Ow!" exclaimed Jonathan. "My shin! Don't move. *Nobody move.* I dropped the TASC control."

"Sorry," said Matt. His eyes were getting used to the dark — now he could see the headstone Jonathan had scraped his shin on. "But hey, we're here! In the Old Burying Ground!"

"I guess all the parts of us made it." Emily sounded a little dazed, unlike her usual lively self. She steadied herself with one hand on a headstone.

Feeling a little dazed himself, Matt took a deep breath. Plowed earth and cow pasture. "It smells like we're in the country, all right." He gazed around the moonlit graveyard, surrounded by a waist-high stone wall. Beyond one end of the graveyard, fields stretched away toward low hills.

"Sounds like the country, too," said Jonathan. Over the peeping of tree frogs, which they were used to hearing at home, a rooster crowed.

"You guys," said Emily in a firmer voice. "We're *here.* We'd better get out to the road, or we'll miss *Paul Revere.*"

"Wait, I have to stow the control." Jonathan slid the TASC control into his leather pouch and tied the pouch to his belt with a careful knot.

"Hold it," Matt told them. "I have to think about which way to go." Turning, he peered at the dim scene around him.

31

At the other end of the graveyard, a cart track led out of a gap in the stone wall. Beyond the wall were two houses, and still farther off, a few more buildings. Somewhere in that direction a dog barked, and a voice called out. Matt pointed. "Okay, the village has to be that way."

The track out of the Old Burying Ground led straight to the Lexington village common. "See that road coming into the village?" asked Matt. "That's the direction Paul Revere's coming from."

"What's going on over there?" Jonathan nodded toward a building on the edge of the common. Yellow light, the only color in the moonlit scene, shone from the first-floor windows. "I thought they went to bed at sundown, in Colonial times."

Matt knew what Jonathan meant. He'd imagined Paul Revere riding around waking the Colonists up, but it seemed they were already wide awake. As they watched, a door opened, and two men stepped out. One of them carried a lantern, which shed a bit of the yellow light from inside.

"That must be Buckman's Tavern," said Matt. "Where the minutemen waited."

"Are waiting," Emily corrected him. Matt caught the breathlessness in her voice, and his own heart skipped a beat. This was the night, *now*. Matt and Emily and Jonathan were here on this rutted, pebbly road in Lexington, in the Massachusetts Bay Colony. In 1775.

Dots of candlelight shone here and there from the small windows of the houses around the common. A small group of men crossed the moonlit grass to the tavern. They greeted the men outside the door and stood talking.

"Listen!" There was a thrill in Emily's voice. "Hoofbeats."

Matt's heart beat faster as he heard the *clop-clop-clop, clop-clop-clop,* from the road past the meetinghouse. "Come on!" Matt started running across the common. "He'll head for that house, the parsonage." He pointed up another road.

As the hoofbeats grew louder, there were shouts behind them. Matt glanced back to see a rider in a three-cornered hat cantering toward the tavern.

"That's him!" breathed Emily.

"What news of the British?" called one of the men in front of the tavern. "Are the Regulars out?"

The Regulars — that meant the British soldiers, Matt remembered.

"Aye," called the man on horseback, passing the tavern without slowing down. Emily and Matt and Jonathan ran on toward the parsonage, but the rider passed them a moment later, in a whiff of horse sweat.

The three kids were pelting after as hard as they could, when suddenly Jonathan put out a long arm to stop the other two. "Get down! Guys with guns."

They dropped behind a stone wall. "Oh, yeah," whispered Matt. "The minutemen put guards around the parsonage, in case the British tried to arrest Hancock and Adams."

As Matt and Emily and Jonathan crouched panting behind the low wall, the rider pulled up in front of the house. A line of men stepped toward him. The barrels of their muskets reflected the moonlight. "Who goes there?"

"Paul Revere, express from the Sons of Liberty in Boston." The rider's voice rang out calm and firm.

Paul Revere. Matt's throat tightened. He felt lucky, so lucky to be right here, right at that moment.

"Reverend Clarke's family is abed, Mr. Revere," said the sentry. "They must not be disturbed by any noise."

"Noise!" exclaimed Revere, swinging off his horse. Out of the saddle, the famous midnight rider looked stockier and not as tall as Matt expected.

"You'll have noise enough before long," Revere was telling the sentry. "The Regulars are marching to arrest Mr. Hancock and Mr. Adams, as well as to seize the stores at Concord." He pushed past the guard and pounded on the door.

Someone shoved open a window on the first floor and stuck his head out. "Come in, Revere. We are not afraid of *you*."

"Who's that, Hancock?" asked someone behind him. "Revere? Good!"

The man behind Hancock must be Samuel Adams, thought Matt. They sure don't sound nervous, for guys in danger of being arrested for treason.

A large man in shirtsleeves opened the door. Revere began, "Reverend Clarke, I am — "

"Welcome, Mr. Revere!" Clarke motioned Revere in the door and gestured to a boy in a nightshirt. The boy ran to take the reins of Revere's horse and lead it off toward the stable.

The parsonage was in a commotion. The sentries called explanations to each other and to Reverend Clarke. Heads, women's and children's, popped out of the upstairs windows, and a baby wailed.

Emily whispered to Matt, "How many people *are* there in that house?" Matt was surprised, too. Somehow he hadn't imagined the Revolution being planned in houses stuffed full of big families.

As Paul Revere disappeared into the house, Reverend Clarke turned to the steep stairway just inside the door. "Children!" he thundered. "Back to your beds!"

The door closed. The house settled down somewhat, although candlelight still glowed from the windows. "Now, what?" asked Jonathan.

"Was that the end of Paul Revere's ride?" asked Emily.

"No, he's going on to Concord." Matt pulled his photocopied map from his pocket and unfolded it. In the moonlight the lines of the roads were clear, although the print was hard to read. "See, here we are in Lexington. This road past the graveyard goes through another village, Lincoln, to Concord. Concord is where the minutemen have their ammunition and cannon and stuff hidden, and the British are marching out from Boston to take it."

A sentry looked their way. "Shh," said Jonathan.

For several minutes the kids stayed crouched behind the wall, waiting for Paul Revere to come out. Matt had a vague, nagging feeling that they were going about this the wrong way. But he wasn't even sure what "this" was, let alone what was wrong with it.

Matt squirmed, trying to ease his cramped leg muscles. He noticed Emily shivering, and wished they'd thought of warmer costumes.

"I'm going to see what he's doing," announced Emily. Matt grabbed at her in horror. But she was already easing over the wall and creeping through the shadows toward a big tree near the house. Peering from around the trunk at the window of a first-story room, she watched for a moment. Then she scuttled noiselessly back.

Matt opened his mouth to scold her, but she spoke first. "They're just sitting around talking. Paul Revere is eating slices of meat and bread and drinking something in a mug — beer, I guess."

Matt shook his head, puzzled. "I'm sure he's going to warn Concord, too."

"What kind of meat?" asked Jonathan. There was a rustle as he pulled something from his pocket, and then a munching sound.

"I'm freezing, just sitting here," said Emily. "Paul Revere probably has to let his horse rest for a while. Why don't we start walking toward the next place he's going to warn?"

"Yeah, I'd like to see that," agreed Jonathan through a mouthful of raisins.

"But that'll take us down the Concord Road," objected Matt. "And besides, this isn't really getting us — "

"Aren't we going to Concord, anyway?" interrupted Emily. "I thought you said there was a big battle there in the morning."

"Yeah, at the North Bridge. But — " Matt was losing his hazy idea about what they were doing wrong. He pulled the map out of his pocket again, to explain that they couldn't walk too far away from Lexington. The first shot of the Revolution would be fired there at sunrise. But now a bell, like a church bell, started clanging nearby.

"Come on." Emily, crouching low, darted away from the wall.

Matt shrugged and folded his map. They might as well see Paul Revere do his thing one more time. As long as they got back to Lexington by dawn . . .

To the urgent clanging of the bell on the common, Matt and Jonathan followed Emily down the road from the parsonage, past the graveyard, and onto the Concord road. Then they walked for some time without talking much. The road rose and dipped and rose again in a hypnotizing rhythm. It wound between pastures and plowed fields, over brooks, past orchards blooming white in the moonlight.

Gradually it came clear to Matt what was bothering him. "Listen," he said finally, "we're never going to find out why the Revolution was fought, this way. We're acting like — well, like we're sightseeing. We should be *talking* to people. You can't tell what somebody's thinking by watching him ride up on a horse."

Emily turned to Matt, astonished. "Yes, you can! *I* could tell, about Paul Revere. Watching him made me feel like — " She spread her hands and rose on her toes, as if she were going to float into the air.

"Yeah, that was cool," agreed Jonathan. But he added in a practical tone, "What we're doing right now, though, I'm not so sure. We must have been walking for a couple of hours."

"At *least*," said Matt as they followed the rutted road into a stand of pines. "Paul Revere should have caught up with us by now." It didn't seem worth trying to explain to Emily and Jonathan what he'd meant about sightseeing. If they went back to Lexington and hung out in the tavern, they'd be doing what he had in mind, anyway. "What if Revere took a shortcut from Lexington and — unh!"

In the tricky scattered light between the trees, Matt had tripped over a root in the road. "All right, that's it," he exclaimed. "We'd better go back to Lexington. We can wait in the tavern until daylight."

"It hasn't been any two hours," said Emily. "You can go back if you want, but I'm not going to. For one thing, it would be silly to walk all this way — "

"We *have* to stick together," Jonathan interrupted her. "I've got the TASC control, and Matt knows the history."

"So what am I, chopped liver?" Emily's voice rose.

"Come on, Em, don't be a pain. We didn't come to 1775 to take a moonlight stroll. Nothing's happening here. There's nobody around."

Even as he said these last words, Matt heard a harness jingle. He was wrong — there was someone straight ahead.

"Halt!" Two men on horseback blocked the road. Men in uniforms, with pistols gleaming in their hands.

"British!" Matt shouted. "Run!"

Jonathan dove into the pine woods on one side of the road. Emily plunged into the underbrush on the other side.

"Halt!" shouted the British officer again.

Blam.

A pistol shot! With his blood pumping through his body at double speed, Matt lunged after Emily. But the lunge stopped short, his right foot caught by another root.

Matt sprawled on the road, grit scraping his palms. The next moment he was picking himself up, encouraged by a hand at the back of his shirt collar and a pistol a few inches from his nose. His heart was still thudding. He felt cold. Would they shoot him, or just beat him up?

"Rouse the countryside against the king's men, will you?" The soldier hauling him up spoke in a low but harsh tone.

The other man laughed scornfully. "It's only a lad, on foot. Take him back to the field with the others, whilst I guard the road."

Handing the reins of his horse to his companion, the first soldier guided Matt, with nudges from his pistol, through the pine trees and into an open space. There were several men on horseback, in pairs: Each man in uniform guarded one man in ordinary clothes. The soldier with Matt gave him a last nudge toward a stump. "Sit down. Hold your tongue."

The nearest prisoner leaned over his horse's neck toward Matt. "Joshua?"

"Hush," growled his British guard. "There's bigger fish swimming toward this net."

Matt sat down on the rough-cut stump, not very comfortably, and rubbed his sore palms against his knee pants. The horse of the nearest prisoner snuffled at his hair. Who was Joshua? More important, what had the British officer meant by "bigger fish"?

Then Matt knew. He sat up, cold and tense. Paul Revere was due to come riding down this road. But maybe Emily or Jonathan were already headed back toward Lexington? They could warn Revere of the British trap.

As Matt strained his ears, there came a faint *clop-clop-clop* from the direction of the road. All the faces of the prisoners and their guards, pale ovals in the dim light, swung toward the sound.

"You are our prisoners, sirs!" There was a scrambled clatter of hooves.

"No, sir, you are ours!" Hoofbeats on the softer ground of a pasture, confused shouting. A horseman burst through the screen of pine trees and into the field where Matt and the rest were guarded.

Two of the British guards spurred their horses to the man's side, and one of them grabbed his reins. "Your name, sir!"

With a sick feeling Matt heard the rider answer. "Paul Revere, sir." Revere's horse hung its head, its sides heaving, but Revere himself sat straight in the saddle. Under his broad forehead, his dark eyes stared steadily at the British soldier.

"You have the temporary advantage of me, sir," Revere went on, "but you are in the gravest danger. I have roused the countryside from here to Boston, and you are cut off from Colonel Smith's Regulars. Indeed, the boats with the troops have grounded in Boston harbor, and they cannot reach Lexington for some hours yet."

The British soldiers stared back at Revere. "Best tell Major Mitchell of this," one of them muttered, and he rode off toward the road.

In a moment an officer on horseback pushed through the pines, the scowl on his face plain even in the moonlight. Major Mitchell, Matt assumed. Matt gasped as the British major shoved a pistol against Revere's head. "By God, sir, if you do not tell me the truth, I will blow your brains out."

To Matt's amazement, Revere let the hint of

a smile curl the corners of his mouth. As if he had the British just where he wanted them, instead of the other way around. The major shot question after question at Revere, but he gave the same calm answers: The boats ferrying the Regulars from Boston to the mainland were stuck in the mud. All the farmers from Lexington to Boston were up in arms — at least five hundred of them would be here in a short while.

Major Mitchell glared at Revere. Then he snapped to his men, "We'll return to Lexington. Put the boy up behind him."

One of the soldiers jumped down and hoisted Matt up behind Paul Revere. "My horse is spent from a night's hard riding," protested Revere.

The major laughed drily. "In that case, sir, you ought not to attempt escape."

Matt, clutching the saddle in front of him, had wildly mixed feelings. On the one hand, he was luckier than he could have dreamed. He'd not only *seen* Revere — he was sharing his horse! On the other hand, the reason Matt was sharing Revere's horse was that they were both prisoners. And the British had loaded down Revere's poor horse with Matt to make sure Revere didn't try to break away.

Two by two the mounted prisoners with their British guards threaded their way through the pines, through a gap in a stone fence, and through more trees to the road. Matt struggled to keep his balance without grabbing the broad back in front of him.

They clopped onto the hard dirt of the road, the major leading Revere's horse by the reins. Paul Revere spoke over his shoulder. "What's your name, boy?"

"Matthew Cowen, sir."

Revere chuckled. "You are no horseman."

"I guess not." Matt was embarrassed. His chance of a lifetime, meeting Paul Revere — and he could hardly keep from falling off his horse.

In a kinder tone Revere went on, "This is a friend's horse, but I can assure you he's a very good horse. You cannot fall off his back, except by a great effort."

This made Matt grin, and he relaxed a little. The horse was still jogging along, but now Matt seemed to be jogging with him instead of against him. "I guess you're right, sir."

"You are not from Middlesex County, Matthew?"

Matt started explaining that he was from the Colony of New York. But the British major leading Revere's horse turned with a cold stare. "I advise you to save your breath, Mr. Revere. You will require it when you stand trial for treason in London."

"No cause for alarm," remarked another officer. "I understand that they seldom execute

44

traitors by drawing and quartering these days."

"On the contrary," another British soldier put in. "The traitor is presented with the finest hempen neckcloth!" He put his fist to the back of his neck and jerked it sharply up, like a hangman's noose.

Matt couldn't see Revere's face, but Revere's broad back, moving easily with the horse, gave no sign that the jibes bothered him. Still, Matt felt so sick, he didn't care whether he fell off the horse or not. How had Paul Revere been captured? Matt had thought he'd ridden all the way to Concord to warn the Colonists. Had something, somehow, gone wrong?

Worse, Matt was a full-fledged idiot, leading his sister and his friend to a place and time where war was about to break out. *War!* And Matt and Emily and Jonathan had come here as if they were visiting Disney World. They hadn't even agreed on where to meet, in case they got separated. Even in Disney World, thought Matt miserably, they'd been *that* careful.

4.
The First Shot

The group of horses with its British soldiers and American prisoners clopped steadily along the dirt road. Matt felt light-headed from staying up so late. The bright moonlight gave the scene the look of a black-and-white movie, or maybe a bad dream. A bad dream in which his rear end was getting sorer and sorer.

Ka-pow. The new sound was distant, but sharply distinct from the hoofbeats, the jingle of harnesses, and the peeping of the tree frogs. *Ka-pow.*

"They're shooting off muskets to sound the alarm," remarked Revere over his shoulder. "In Lexington, or maybe Lincoln. Doubtless the Concord bell is clanging, too, although we're too far away to hear it."

Matt sat up straighter. "Concord? But how would they know the British were coming, in Concord?"

Revere turned again, one eyebrow raised in

46

amusement. "Did you think I was the only express rider, lad?"

"Oh," said Matt. Of course the patriots would send out more than one messenger, so that the warning would be sure to get through.

"For one," Revere went on, "Dr. Prescott escaped this patrol. He'd be in Concord by now."

Matt felt lighter. "Maybe I could do something to help *you* escape, sir. I could yell and fall off the horse to distract their attention, or — " Matt stopped talking as several more musket shots went off in the distance.

Major Mitchell reined in his horse and Revere's, and the patrol halted while Mitchell peered down the road. "What is that infernal noise for?"

"Why, it's to alarm the countryside," answered Revere in a helpful tone. "The militia number five hundred in Lexington alone."

"Damned rebels." The major stared from one side of the road to the other, squinting at a stone wall as if there must be a row of minutemen behind it.

Then the British officer snapped orders. All the prisoners except Revere and Matt dismounted. Cutting the extra horses' bridles and saddle girths, the soldiers drove them up the road toward Concord. The Colonists, too, were chased up the road with threats.

Remounting, the patrol rode on at a faster

pace, with Revere and Matt in the middle. Matt was sure the British had overlooked him, half-hidden in the dark behind Revere's stocky form. They were keeping Revere, of course, because he was the most important prisoner. If Matt had made himself noticed, they would have let him go, too.

But I'm not really sorry, thought Matt. And if Mr. Revere isn't worried, why should I be?

After a moment, Revere turned his head. "What's the mood in New York, young Matthew? It's some months since I rode there."

"Well . . ." Matt thought over what he knew about his local history. "There are a lot of Tories in our town."

"No doubt," said Revere. "There are many Colonists who think the cause of liberty is treason." In a kind tone he asked, "Is your father a Tory, Matthew?"

"Oh, no. He's a patriot." Thinking of his father and Mr. Kingsley, Matt added, "But my father has to do business with the British sometimes."

Revere shrugged. "No disloyalty in that — British silver can be put to the work of liberty."

Bong . . . bong . . . bong. A bell, like the one Matt and Emily and Jonathan had heard earlier, was clanging not too far away. The major halted again, looking tenser than before. "We must make haste, without the burden of prisoners." He glared at Revere. "I deeply regret I am unable to escort you to prison. Dismount, sir."

Matt's heart thudded. Were the British letting Revere and Matt go — or were they going to shoot them on the spot?

Swinging off his horse, Revere gave Matt a hand down. The hint of a smile curled Revere's mouth again.

A soldier pulled out a knife to cut the bridle of Revere's horse, but the major held up his hand. "No. This is a better horse than Sergeant Jones's. Sergeant — " He jerked his head from one of his men to Revere's horse.

As the sergeant remounted, Matt was surprised to see Paul Revere looking disturbed for the first time. "The horse is already weary," he protested. "Besides, it belongs to Mr. Larkin of Charlestown."

The sergeant laughed. "Give my best regards to Mr. Larkin. And thank him for the use of his fine rebel horse — only for the night, to be sure."

The rest of the patrol laughed, too. Major Mitchell turned his horse's head down the road and led them away at a canter.

As the British disappeared around a bend, Revere sighed. "Such a fine horse. That's the last John Larkin or any of us will see of him, you may wager." Then he beckoned to Matt, speaking briskly. "Come, we'll cut across the fields to the village."

Following Paul Revere, Matt jumped over a ditch beside the road, vaulted a stone wall, and stumbled across rows of furrows. Revere waited beside another wall for Matt to catch up. "Did you mark how the major swallowed my tale about the Regulars running aground in the harbor — swallowed it at one gulp!" His teeth flashed white as he laughed. "And did you see the major's face when he heard the musket shots? What do you think was in his mind — hundreds — no, *thousands* — of maddened countrymen, coming at him with pitchforks?" He plunged on across the next field, chuckling.

Matt laughed, too, mostly from relief. A moment ago they'd been on their way to prison — now, just like that, they were free.

After several minutes of trudging over someone's farm, Matt recognized the rows of headstones on the other side of a wall. "We must be in back of the Old Burying Ground."

"The burying ground, yes," said Revere, giving Matt an odd look. "Not so very old." He passed the back of the graveyard and picked his way around a swamp to a road. "I'm returning to the parsonage, to make sure Hancock and Adams escaped safely. Fare well, Matthew."

Fare well? That was it? Watching Revere cross the road, Matthew felt let down and suddenly tired. But before he could say good-bye,

Revere stopped and turned. "Matthew. You wish to aid the cause of liberty?"

"Yes," said Matt quickly.

"Then go to Buckman's Tavern" — Revere pointed up the road toward the common — "and ask for Captain John Parker. Tell him of the events on the Concord road tonight." Another wave, and Revere was off across the fields again.

"Good-bye, sir," called Matt. He was disappointed that Paul Revere hadn't asked him to come along and help *him*. But that was just as well, he realized as he headed toward the tavern. He'd gotten a little carried away. The first thing he had to do now was find Emily and Jonathan.

As Matt walked toward the yellow-lit windows of the tavern, a hopeful thought occurred to him. Maybe Emily and Jonathan were already there, waiting for him. That would make sense, wouldn't it? Just before they ran into the British patrol, Matt had been explaining that they should go back to Lexington and wait in the tavern until dawn.

As Matt lifted the iron latch of the tavern door, he expected to see Emily's and Jonathan's faces turn toward him. But the crowd in the low-raftered room were all men. The air, thick with wood smoke and tobacco smoke, made Matt sneeze.

Only a few casual glances were cast at Matt

as he eased his way into the tavern, dimly lit by candles on the walls. There was a hum of talk from the men sitting on benches or standing in groups. A man with heavy eyebrows and a quick smile worked behind the bar, greeting customers and pouring drink into pewter or wooden mugs and chalking up tabs on the wall in back of him. Since the tavern keeper seemed to know everyone by name, Matt stepped up to the bar and asked where he could find Captain Parker. Without pausing in his work, the man nodded toward the fireplace on the other side of the room.

Approaching the group in front of the fireplace, Matt picked out a middle-aged man with a sensible, fatherly face. "Excuse me, sir. I'm looking for Captain Parker."

A short, young man in the group grinned, as if Matt had said something funny. But the fatherly man simply took his long-stemmed pipe from his mouth. "You've found him, boy."

Explaining that Paul Revere had sent him, Matt told about their capture by the British patrol.

Captain Parker nodded thoughtfully. "The other prisoners must have been some of our scouts." He nodded again, then added, "Well done, boy." He spoke to the short young man. "Joshua, get a mug of cider for young Matthew. Put it on my reckoning."

A moment later Joshua returned from the bar with a full mug. But instead of handing it to Matt, he pulled a poker from the fire and stuck it into the cider with a sizzle.

"Whoa, what are you doing?" protested Matt.

Joshua looked up in surprise. "Don't you like it hot?"

Matt felt confused. "Sure, but — " He'd imagined the cider simmering in a pot, but it seemed they heated drinks in a different way in Buckman's Tavern. Stepping forward to take the mug, he stumbled on an uneven floorboard.

Laughing, Joshua steadied Matt with a hand on his arm. "You're rambling like a lost calf! Better have a rest on the settle." He motioned Matt into a high-backed bench beside the fireplace.

Matt felt foolish, but he also realized how tired he really was. As he sat down, he remembered the other thing he'd come to the tavern for. "You haven't seen my — er — brother and my friend, have you?" he asked Joshua. "A younger boy with red hair and a tall, skinny boy?"

Joshua shook his head as he turned back to join the group. "No strangers but you."

Leaning back in a corner of the settle, Matt sipped his cider. It tasted a little like ashes, but who cared. He was cold and tired, and the cider was warm and sweet. Matt couldn't see the door from where he sat, but he could hear it bang shut every few minutes as men came and went. He looked up each time, hoping to see Emily and Jonathan step into the dim, flickering light.

Meanwhile, Matt listened to the conversation of the men by the fire. "They say General Gage is sending out three thousand troops against us," declared one man, wide-eyed.

The man next to him gave him a scornful look. "Mr. Revere, direct from Dr. Warren in Boston, says seven hundred — don't you suppose he knows?"

An older man pulled his pipe from his mouth to speak up. "I don't care if they've sent *ten* thousand — I'm not a-running from the red-coats."

"The question," said Captain Parker quietly, "is not how many, but *when*. I'd have thought one of the couriers would have returned with news, by now."

Slumped back on the settle, Matt caught bits of talk about old battles in the French and Indian Wars, about what bad shots the British Regulars were. One man grumbled that he ought to be starting his spring plowing tomorrow.

Matt wasn't aware of dozing off, but he opened his eyes with a start as someone joggled the settle. It was Joshua, leaning back in the opposite corner.

"We may as well sleep, eh?" He gave an enormous yawn. "The Regulars will be here soon enough."

Matt thought at first that Joshua was showing off, acting as if the battle coming up was no big deal to him. But within a few minutes Joshua seemed genuinely asleep, with his head on his chest and his mouth open.

He's probably had a hard day's work in the fields, thought Matt. Of course, Matt himself had had a hard day's time travel. But he intended to stay awake now, and keep an eye out for Emily and Jonathan. The last thing he remembered was setting down his cider mug.

Matt woke up to a steady rattle. Somewhere outside, but too loud to ignore. They shouldn't be making all that noise, he thought indignantly, when people are trying to sleep.

Then the settle shook as Joshua scrambled to his feet. Matt's eyes popped open, and his heart started pumping briskly. He was in Lexington in April, 1775. The redcoats were coming.

"They're playing 'to arms,'" said Joshua. He nodded toward the rattle, which Matt realized now was a drumroll.

As Joshua headed for the door, Matt lifted himself stiffly from the hard settle. There was light outside the tavern window — not moonlight, but the faint orange of dawn. On the common, the bell began to clang again.

Inside the tavern there was a quiet, serious buzz of activity. Men pulled on their shoes, and checked their ammunition. The old man Matt had noticed last night muttered as he loaded his musket. *"I'm* not a-running from the redcoats, no matter what."

Following the men out of the tavern, Matt stood blinking in the sunlight. Across the road and farther down the common, Captain Parker was lining up his troops. The young drummer boy beat out the same signal over and over. Men hurried onto the trampled ground and stepped into the lines.

But still, thought Matt with a shock, there aren't more than fifty of them. Against *seven hundred?*

"We're short on powder." It was Joshua, near the tavern door, speaking to two other young men. "Best fetch a keg from the meetinghouse before — " He motioned up the flat stretch of road past the meetinghouse.

That was the road on which the British were marching, Matt knew. His empty stomach did a flip.

The other young men had started for the meetinghouse when Joshua's eye fell on Matt. "Come along with us, boy. You can carry a musket or two." Joshua trotted after his companions, across the common and toward the front door of the meetinghouse. Matt ran after them.

Inside, there were rows of pews facing the pulpit and the back door. The men's feet pounded the wooden floor as they hurried around the pews to the barrels and kegs and clusters of muskets against the back wall. Joshua and the others lifted kegs to their shoulders and headed for the front door.

Matt tried to take an armful of muskets, as if they were skis. But the muskets weren't just long — they were heavy. He managed three and followed the men, staggering.

Suddenly he saw bright red outside the front windows. The color halted Matt like a traffic light.

The young men whirled and ran for the back door, still carrying the kegs. Matt ran awkwardly after them. The man in the lead yanked open the door — and stopped short again.

Rows of scarlet uniforms filled the road between them and the tavern. The rising sun flashed from tidy rows of bayonets. The redcoats were pouring into the space between the meetinghouse and the two thin lines of Lexington minutemen.

Joshua growled, and Matt felt an answering surge of anger. The redcoats had no right to be here. Matt might not be from Lexington or 1775, but he was American. And they were the enemy.

A British officer, on horseback beside the foot

soldiers, called out to his troops. "Surround and disarm them!"

As the red lines moved forward, the officer turned to shout to Captain Parker's farmers. "Lay down your arms!"

"Never," muttered the youth in the doorway.

Farther down the common, Captain Parker called out something to his men. The Lexington drummer played a new rhythm. " 'Disperse,' " interpreted Joshua.

In ones and twos the minutemen turned out of their straggly lines and started to walk away. Except for a stooped figure: the old man who wasn't "a-running from the redcoats."

Matt held his breath. He seemed to feel the three men in front of him, and all the onlookers near Buckman's Tavern and around the common, holding theirs. Surely there was no reason for the British troops, hundreds of them, to attack those few farmers as they walked off the common.

A shot cracked. From where? Matt couldn't tell.

But in answer, the rows of British muskets went off like a string of firecrackers. Stabs of fire burst from the musket barrels, then puffs of smoke. The redcoats surged forward, yelling, their bayonets level.

"Run for Munroe's," gasped the young man in the doorway. He lunged out the meetinghouse door and bolted across the common, toward a house opposite the tavern. The next man dashed after him.

A musket ball *zinged* into the door frame of the meetinghouse. Matt flinched. But he stood there as if his feet were glued to the spot, clutching the muskets in his arms and staring through the blue gunsmoke. At the edge of the common, the first man out of the meetinghouse fell. The second man staggered as if a ball had hit him, but he kept running.

A British officer rode among the stampeding redcoats, his face furious. Over and over he swung his sword down in a signal. "Cease fire!" he screamed above the din. "Damn you, cease fire!" No one paid any attention.

Then Matt was jerked out of the doorway by his arm, and Joshua banged the door shut. "If the redcoats come after our powder — we'll give it to them." He laughed shortly and grabbed one of the muskets from Matt.

At first, Matt thought Joshua meant he'd shoot any British soldier who came through the door. Matt wished he knew how to use a gun, so he could back Joshua up.

But then Matt saw what Joshua was doing. Ripping the top off a powder keg, the young man dumped a charge of powder into the musket. Then he lay down on the floor, out of sight of the windows. He motioned Matt to do the same.

Turning the powder keg on its side, Joshua shoved the muzzle of his musket into the gunpowder.

Matt's heart seemed to stop beating. He dropped onto the rough planks of the floor. The yelling and trampling and shots outside sounded very close. If the redcoats came in that door, Joshua would fire into the gunpowder. He'd blow them all up.

Now, too late, Matt knew what he wished he'd told Mr. Kingsley: *These Colonists wouldn't risk dying over a dumb thing like taxes. They were fighting for each other. For the right to run their own lives.*

Muscles in Joshua's jaw stood out in knots as he stared at the door. For an instant his gaze flicked aside, meeting Matt's. "Be brave, boy."

5.
Spreading the Alarm

Emily didn't see Matt get captured by the British patrol. She was scrambling through the underbrush, straight away from the road, still hearing that earsplitting pistol shot.

Emily thought Matt was right behind her until she paused, out of breath, to listen. Did she hear voices, back toward the road? It was hard to tell. Her own breathing was so loud, and the tree frogs had started up their peeping chorus again.

"Matt?" said Emily softly. "Jonathan?" There was no answer.

After calling and waiting, calling and waiting again, Emily decided to go back to the road. Not where the British patrol had surprised them, of course, but farther on toward Concord, where they were going anyway. Matt and Jonathan must be ahead of her after all, on the road by now.

Trying not to make too much noise, Emily

wove her way around trees and thickets and boulders. She crawled over logs and jumped a little stream. After several minutes, she thought she must be well past the British patrol. Turning, she walked as straight as she could toward where she thought the road must be. She stepped out of trees into a field. Sure enough, the white moonlit curve of the road lay beyond the stone wall.

Emily listened again. No footsteps. Matt and Jonathan must be way ahead of her. She hurried down the road. At first she stopped to listen every few minutes, but there was no sound except the *peep-peep-peep* of the tree frogs and the rustling of dry leaves.

Emily walked on and on. Not knowing the road, or where Matt and Jonathan were on it, she couldn't tell how fast she was getting wherever it was she wanted to go. In the bright eerie moonlight, by herself, she started to have the feeling that she was walking along the same stretch of road, through the same fields and woods and swamps, over and over.

But here, at last, was something different: a house. A small white house on a hill, with outbuildings in back of it. Was this one of the families Paul Revere would wake up and warn? Maybe she should wait and see. No — she had to catch up with Matt and Jonathan.

Remembering Paul Revere riding into Lexington, Emily felt a pang of envy. Somehow, without really thinking about it, she'd expected to be on horseback herself. Of course that was silly — horses in Colonial times weren't just running around loose for anyone to ride, any more than people in her time could drive off with anyone's car.

Emily loved horses. The saddest day of her life was when her father told her she couldn't keep on with riding lessons, because they couldn't afford it. When she was older, she'd earn the money herself.

Trudging over a rise and down into a dip, Emily caught sight of another farmhouse near the road. This house was larger and a dark color. The clapboards covering the walls looked like corduroy in the moonlight. Behind the black-windowed house and barn, fields spread out.

What was that? Emily stood still to listen. A rustling in the woods beyond the fields, like a large animal pushing through the underbrush. The next moment, a horse and rider burst out of a thicket and trotted past the barn to the back door of the house.

Paul Revere? But this horse and rider didn't look quite like the ones who'd cantered up to the parsonage in Lexington.

The man pounded on the door of the farmhouse. "Samuel Hartwell! Mary Hartwell! The Regulars are out!" A few seconds, then an answering voice. A faint yellow light shone from the downstairs windows, and the door opened. A man appeared on the doorstep.

The two spoke in low tones. Then the rider turned his horse and trotted toward the road. Catching sight of Emily, he called, "The Regulars are out! Spread the alarm." Pebbles scattered as he cantered off in the direction of Concord.

Emily stood on the road staring after him. She forgot about being tired of walking and worried about where Matt and Jonathan were. *Spread the alarm.* Yes!

She wanted to help. It wasn't right for the three kids from the future to come here, where people were fighting for their freedom, and just watch as if it were some TV program. She had to find out how she could help.

Emily hurried around to the back door of the farmhouse. She had to knock several times before the latch clicked inside and the door opened. A young woman with her hair in a long braid and a shawl around her shoulders held up a candle, shedding a circle of yellow light. "Who's there?"

This was Mary Hartwell, Emily guessed. "Mrs. Hartwell, I'm Em — " Emily remembered in time that she was dressed like a boy. "I'm Ethan — "

"Ethan Bennett?" The woman peered at Emily

as if she almost recognized her. "To be sure, you're the cousin from Deerfield. The Deerfield Bennetts have that strain for red hair."

As Emily wondered whether to play along with this or not, Mrs. Hartwell went on. "But I've no time for chatter. Did you not hear Dr. Prescott just now? The British are marching from Boston to seize the stores of arms at Concord. Mr. Hartwell must join the Lincoln minutemen, and I must spread the alarm."

"I know," said Emily eagerly. "Please let me help."

Giving Emily a thoughtful look, Mary Hartwell stepped back from the door to let her into the kitchen. The room smelled like stale ashes.

"Indeed, I believe you can help me, Ethan." As the woman turned, Emily noticed two small forms shuffling beside her. Two wide-eyed little girls clung to Mary Hartwell's skirts.

Mary moved around the kitchen, lighting more candles from the one in her hand. Objects in the room sprang into view: a spinning wheel, a round table, a hooded cradle near the fireplace. Whimpering came from the cradle, and Mary rocked it with one foot. At the same time, she threw kindling into the fireplace, poked it, and puffed air at it with a bellows until it burst into flame. She lifted the lid of an iron pot hanging in the fireplace and stirred the pot.

Then Mary Hartwell put her hands on her

hips and looked down at her older girl, about four. "Polly, you must be a big, brave girl for a short while. Father makes haste to join the minutemen. Mother must run to Captain Smith's and tell him the redcoats are coming. *You* must help Ethan mind Sally and the baby. You know how to rock the baby if she cries, don't you?"

Tears welling from her eyes, Polly clutched her mother's skirt harder than ever. "Don't go, Muzzer! The redcoats will get me."

"Wedcoaths," repeated the younger sister. Her mouth turned down. The baby began to squeak.

Mary blew out her breath in frustration. "So I am paid back, for frightening them to be good with tales of redcoats. Polly, listen to — "

"Hey, why don't I go warn Captain Smith?" interrupted Emily. "Where does he live?"

Mary Hartwell shook her head. "Captain Smith does not know you. I must go myself, after I say a word to Mr. Hartwell."

The little girls stumbled after their mother, still holding onto her skirts, as she went to the door of the next room and spoke in low tones to her husband. Back at the fireplace, Mary pried the little hands from the folds of her dress. "Be good, brave children. I'll be back soon." She wrapped herself in a cloak, and the door closed behind her.

Polly and Sally looked doubtfully at Emily, and she looked doubtfully at them. Baby-sitting was not the way she'd intended to help the Revolution. The littler sister started to sob again. "Wedcoaths." Polly stared at Emily with her lip trembling. The baby whimpered.

"Come on, Polly, rock the baby so she won't cry. Or do I have to do it?" Emily bent down, putting one hand on the rocker of the cradle.

Polly hesitated, then stooped beside the cradle and pushed Emily's hand away. "This is *my* baby sister, Lucy." As she rocked, the baby's whimpers trailed off.

That takes care of two of them, thought Emily. But Sally toddled over to her older sister and grabbed her nightgown. "Wedcoath!" she wailed.

Polly let go of the rocker. "I want Muzzer."

Oh, man, thought Emily. It would be easier to comfort these kids if she didn't know they were right to be afraid. For all Emily knew, Samuel Hartwell might be one of the first patriots to die for the American cause. And what if Mary were shot by a British patrol, like the one that surprised Emily and Matt and Jonathan?

Letting out a sigh, Emily pushed her hands into her pockets — and felt the lump of raisins. "Hey. Polly — do you like raisins?"

Polly looked puzzled, but she and Sally stopped crying and watched as Emily pulled the handkerchief from her pocket. Polly peered in, and a look of wonder broke over her round face. "It's plums, Sally!"

The girls held out cupped hands, their little fingers wiggling eagerly. One at a time, with great concentration, they ate the raisins Emily placed in their palms. Even Sally didn't drop a single raisin.

As Polly held out her hands for more, she said proudly, *"We* had a plum pudding, at Christmas."

A man somewhat older than Mary stepped into the kitchen from the next room, pulling on a gray coat. "Ethan," he greeted Emily with a nod, but he seemed intent on his preparations. He filled a sack with half a loaf of bread, a chunk of cheese, some small pieces of cloth, and a few utensils. He tied a powder horn to his belt. His little daughters silently watched every move, chewing their raisins.

The latch of the door lifted, and Mary Hartwell appeared. She looked relieved, Emily thought proudly, to see that her kids weren't bawling their heads off with the strange "boy." As she hung up her cloak and tied on an apron, Mary spoke to her husband. "William Smith was awake — he expected the news." She stepped to the fireplace and ladled mush from the pot into a wooden bowl. "You'll break fast before you leave?"

"Aye." Samuel Hartwell put down his sack

and sat at the kitchen table long enough to eat his cornmeal mush. Emily gave him raisins to sprinkle on it, and Hartwell's serious face broke into a grin. "You must fear I'll weep, too, unless you stop my mouth with plums."

Actually, Emily was surprised at how calm Mary and Samuel Hartwell were acting. She caught a flash of worry in his eyes only when he said good-bye. "You'll take the children to your father's after daylight, then?" he said to Mary. "The redcoats will not come to the center of Lincoln."

Samuel Hartwell kissed each of his three little girls and his wife. Then he lifted his battered musket from pegs on the wall, and he was out the door and gone.

Pressing her lips together, Mary blinked rapidly. Emily had been imagining her own mother saying good-bye to her own father going off to war, and she wouldn't have blamed Mary if she had burst out sobbing.

But the young woman only dabbed her eyes with the hem of her apron. Then she led the little girls into the next room and tucked them into bed. Back in the kitchen, Mary took two wooden bowls from a shelf. "*We* will not sleep again to-night. Let us break fast." She pulled the cradle over to the table, to rock it with one foot while they ate.

Emily wasn't sure she'd like corn mush. But

she was hungry, and she had a feeling she'd better eat while she could. Actually the hot cereal tasted better than she expected, with her raisins and fresh, sweet milk on it. Emily ate two bowlfuls, and drank a mug of the odd tea Mary brewed from blackberry leaves.

"This is not the king's tea, with its shameful tax," she assured Emily.

Mary ate as if she was thinking hard about something, frowning toward the fire. "Ethan," she said finally, "the Regulars may arrive before we are ready to leave for my father's. If we see they mean us harm, we must run into the woods. I will carry the baby and take Polly by the hand, while you carry Sally."

"Okay . . ." Emily felt as if the mush had suddenly lumped up in her stomach. "The British soldiers — they'd attack women and children?"

"They may intend to burn our house down," said Mary grimly. "The Tory spies may have told them that Mr. Hartwell is a patriot and a gunsmith. He has repaired all the minutemen's muskets in Lincoln, and more besides."

Emily didn't scare easily, but now she felt afraid for Mary Hartwell and her children. "Maybe you should leave right away."

Mary glanced out the window, where it was lighter now than in the candlelit kitchen. "After chores." First she got the little girls up and gave them breakfast. Then she went to milk the cows and hitch the horse to the cart.

Watching the children for Mary again, Emily remembered the way Mr. Kingsley had talked about the Colonists. "Peasants," he'd called them. Meaning *stupid, ignorant.* Mary and Samuel Hartwell might live a simple life, but they weren't dumb. They knew what they were doing. They were brave.

Mary came back from chores, pinned up her hair, and put on a ruffled cap. Emily was helping her dress Polly and Sally when they heard a new sound in the distance. Mary drew in her breath sharply. The new sound, Emily realized, was hundreds of feet hitting the ground at the same time. *Tramp, tramp, tramp.*

They all ran to the front of the house and peered out the windows. From the direction of Lexington, a stream of scarlet uniforms poured over the rise. The color was shocking, against the soft grays and browns and greens of the April countryside. The upright bayonets threw flashes of sunlight from side to side as the soldiers marched.

Mary looked awestruck. "If I didn't know what they came for," she whispered, "I'd say that was the finest sight I'd ever seen in my life."

Emily stared at the British soldiers in their high pointed caps and white leggings, swinging along so precisely. She imagined them marching past *her* house as if they owned the place. She couldn't see their faces well, but they all seemed to look like George Kingsley. She thought of Samuel Hartwell in his homemade gray and brown clothes, and his musket with the dented barrel.

In spite of Mary's fears, the British marched past the Hartwells' without stopping. Mary let out a long sigh and led her children back through the house to the kitchen door. "We must go to Grandfather's now, before the redcoats come back." She laid a hand on Emily's arm. "Ethan, you must wish to return to the Bennetts'. Tell them Mary Hartwell was glad of your help this night."

"Actually, I was on my way to Concord," said Emily, thinking glumly of the miles she still had to trudge. As they stepped out the back door, her eye fell on an extra horse tied behind the cart. "Whoa! Are you going to be using that horse today? I mean, could I ride him to Concord?"

Mary seemed glad to do "Ethan" a favor. She untied the horse and showed Emily the saddle and other gear in the barn. "Do not ride Dancer into the village, mind," she warned as Emily shortened the stirrups. "The king's troops are great thieves and would take a horse without a by-your-leave. I have it!" she exclaimed. "You may leave Dancer with my cousin Hannah. Her farm is near Concord, but not on the main road or in the village."

When the children were settled in the cart behind Mary, and Emily was mounted on Dancer, Mary gave her directions to Cousin Hannah's. Emily waved as Mary drove the cart onto the road.

Polly and Sally, wearing little cloaks like their mother's, waved back. "Plums!" called Sally. Mary turned the cart down a side road, and then the Hartwells were hidden from Emily's sight by a row of pines.

6.
The Redcoats' Breakfast

In spite of not sleeping at all the night before, Emily felt great. The early morning sun was shining on her back, the fields and woods were fresh with the faint green of spring, and she was riding a wonderful horse.

Dancer was small and stringy, with a grayish-brown coat that Mary Hartwell had called dun. But he was light on his feet, and there was an eager gleam in his eyes. So different from the bored, lumpish horses at the stable where Emily had taken riding lessons.

On horseback, it shouldn't take long at all to get to Concord, even though Emily would have to walk the last stretch into the village. Then she'd look for Matt and Jonathan at the North Bridge. They'd both head there, she was sure, because that's where the battle would take place. And they knew *she* knew that, so they'd look for her, too.

As Emily and her borrowed horse trotted down the rutted road, Dancer flicked his ears back to listen to her. "I bet *you* know the way," she told him. "Let's see, Mrs. Hartwell said we'd go up a steep hill, like this . . . and then down the back of the hill, with rocky slopes on both sides. And there's the big dead tree where we're supposed to — "

Emily stiffened in the saddle. Far down the road, disappearing around a bend and another hill, was a flash of scarlet. She pulled Dancer up, her heart tripping. She'd almost caught up with the British troops.

After waiting until she was sure they were gone, Emily rode past the dead tree and turned onto a path beside a stone wall. The path faded in and out, twisting this way and that.

Here and there Emily spotted men in drab-colored clothes, in twos and threes, carrying muskets. They were all hurrying in the same direction: toward Concord, like Emily.

All too soon for Emily, she reached Cousin Hannah's farm and the ride was over. Hannah herself, a young woman with tired eyes, burped a baby on her shoulder as she gave Emily directions to the village. "But the Regulars march for Concord," she warned. "Had you not better wait here until they leave?"

"I'll be careful." Emily waved and hurried

down the path Cousin Hannah had pointed out. She'd better run, now, to make sure she got into Concord before the British.

Emily was soon on the road that would bring her into Concord. "Keep on the road all the way to the gristmill in the village," Hannah had said. "Then you'll spy the courthouse, a great white building. The road opposite leads to the North Bridge."

Emily ran, then walked to catch her breath, then ran again. She passed wandering pigs on the road, and cows and horses and oxen in the pastures. No one was working in the fields, although she noticed a plow left in the middle of a furrow. It seemed that everyone in Concord was either staying out of sight of the redcoats, or rushing to fight them.

Finally Emily came to a long pond with a cluster of buildings on the other side. Yellow-green willows dipped their branches into the water. On one end of the pond was a mill with a huge wheel. The wheel was still — no one was grinding flour today.

Crossing the road over the mill dam, Emily stopped and looked around the village common. Nearby was a reddish-brown tavern with a swinging sign out in front. Beyond the tavern stood a barnlike building, like the meetinghouse in Lexington. And over there was the "great white building" Hannah had mentioned — the courthouse. That road across the common must lead to the North Bridge, where she'd look for Matt and Jonathan.

"Here, boy!"

Emily turned, not really thinking anyone was talking to her — although there was no one else in the square.

An older girl, wearing a brown dress with an apron and a ruffled cap, strode out of the tavern. "The Regulars will be here any minute — you must help to hide the last of the stores." The girl had round blue eyes and slightly buck teeth that gave her a rabbity look, but she grabbed Emily's arm in a determined way.

"Hey," protested Emily as she was yanked toward the tavern. That girl was stronger than she looked. "Let me go — I have to find my older brother."

The older girl gave an impatient laugh. "Are you soft in the head? Your brother is no doubt up by the Liberty Pole with the minutemen." She waved toward a steep hill across the common. "Unless you are Tories." She shot Emily a narrow glance.

"Of course we aren't Tories! We're patriots." Emily gazed up at the hill, dotted with headstones like the Lexington graveyard. A flag waved at the top of the hill.

In between the headstones, the hill was covered with men in broad-brimmed farmer's hats, carrying muskets. Samuel Hartwell might be up on that hill, thought Emily. And maybe Matt *was* there, too — she saw a few minutemen in shirtsleeves. Maybe he'd gotten caught up in helping the Colonists, the way Emily had.

The men were all staring in the same direction — up another road that led into the common. The thin tweetling of a fife floated on the spring breeze.

"Do you hear?" demanded the older girl. "The redcoats, or my name's not Abigail Chandler. Make haste!" She pulled Emily in the tavern door.

Emily stopped struggling and went along. Clearly this wasn't a good time to try to find Matt and Jonathan. And besides, she did want to help.

Inside the taproom, Abigail stood Emily at the bar. She showed her a small keg of musket balls and a row of square green bottles. "As fast as you can fill them, put the gin bottles in the case behind the bar." She rushed off into a back room, and Emily heard scraping and thumping sounds.

Emily started scooping handfuls of the lead beads, the size of blueberries, from the keg. They poured into the bottles with a heavy rattle. When each bottle was corked and stowed in the wooden box in a dark corner, they looked as if they could be full of liquor.

"Are you done?" demanded Abigail, rushing

back into the room. "Here, help me carry this up to the garret."

"This" was a long, heavy bundle wrapped in hide and tied with thongs. Emily took one end, and at a wave from the older girl, she began to back up the steep stairs. "What's in here?"

"Curiosity killed the cat," said Abigail with an innocent rabbity smile. "Muskets," she added. She pushed Emily with the bundle into a room under the eaves, so low that they both had to duck. "Quick, slide it under my bed."

Giving the long bundle a last shove with her heel, Abigail straightened and stood still. "Listen."

It was the same sound Emily had listened to with Mary Hartwell: the tramp of hundreds of feet.

Abigail clattered down the stairs, with Emily after her. They reached the front doorway of the tavern in time to see row after row of scarlet-coated soldiers march into the square.

When the common was full of troops, a fat officer on horseback shouted an order. His second-in-command repeated it, and a section of rows detached itself from the ranks. These soldiers began to climb the steep hill on the other side of the common. The minutemen, Emily noticed, had disappeared.

Emily couldn't see what the British were doing up on the hill, but she could hear a rhythmic ringing sound. Then there was a loud crack, and the flag fell out of sight.

"How dare they," muttered Abigail. Her blue eyes looked hard. "How *dare* they chop down our Liberty Pole."

On the other side of the common, the fat officer called out another command. The man beside him echoed it, and another group of soldiers detached from the troops in the square. They marched down the road opposite the courthouse — the road to the North Bridge.

"They know where the stores are hidden, right enough," said Abigail grimly.

"But we hid them here," said Emily.

The girl gave her a pitying look, as if Emily had just proved she *was* soft in the head. "The balls and muskets we hid are only a bit of the stores. Most of them are at Barrett's farm, across the North Bridge."

"Off to Barrett's, are they, Abigail?" said a man's voice behind them.

Abigail turned and curtsied to a middle-aged man in shirtsleeves and an apron. "Aye, Mr. Wright. I suppose a spy must have told the British."

"A cursed Tory spy." Mr. Wright brushed dirt off his hands as he spoke. "Well, let them search here if they like. At least my silver is safely buried in the yard."

"And this boy and I have hid the balls and

muskets, sir." Abigail nodded toward Emily, adding in a whisper, "He's slow, but biddable."

The tavern keeper took a closer look at Emily. "This isn't a Concord boy, unless I'm greatly mistaken."

"Ethan Bennett, sir," said Emily boldly, remembering Mary Hartwell's mistake. "From Deerfield."

Mr. Wright gave a grunt of recognition, his gaze resting on Emily's red hair. "Aye, the Deerfield Bennetts." He clapped Emily on the shoulder. "Well, then, Ethan. Work hard, and you'll have your dinner and a new penny for your pains."

Emily swallowed a smart answer about the penny. "Thank you, sir."

Out in the square, the fat officer was shouting orders again. Soldiers broke off in small groups and spread out in different directions. One group headed straight for the Wright Tavern.

Close up, these soldiers were tall, and their pointed caps made them seem even taller. Emily stared at their sharp, shiny bayonets, longer than her arm.

Emily felt like slamming the tavern door on the invaders, but Mr. Wright swung it wide open. He smiled broadly. "Good morning, sirs. What is your pleasure? I have cold pork and fried ham, boiled potatoes, new-baked bread — "

One of the soldiers, a friendly looking fellow

with little brown eyes, licked his lips. But the officer in charge cut Mr. Wright short. "Innkeeper, we come to search for military stores, not breakfast." He spoke to the man who seemed so interested in food. "Roberts, inspect the upstairs."

"I'll show the way," said Abigail in a helpful tone, hurrying ahead. From the staircase came her clear, carrying voice. "Here you see the guest rooms. And above, my garret."

"Are there only your private possessions above?" asked the soldier politely.

"Yes, only my poor belongings." Abigail's tone managed to say that it would be unbelievably mean — *ungentlemanly* — for him to search her room.

"I need not disturb them, then," said Roberts.

Emily looked at the floor to hide her surprise. This redcoat was going to take Abigail's word for it? What kind of a search was that?

Meanwhile, the other soldiers and their officer poked around the taproom and the parlor and the kitchen in back. Emily held her breath as one of the men looked behind the bar. But his gaze swept over the case of gin bottles without pausing.

Roberts returned from upstairs, and now they all wanted breakfast. Mr. Wright poured drinks, while Abigail worked in the kitchen. Emily, with an apron tied around her waist, served the redcoats wooden plates full of food.

"Put a loaf on each table," Abigail told her, pointing out the bread in a basket on the kitchen table. She giggled. "Did you note, Mr. Wright called it new-baked? To be sure, it *was* new-baked, last Saturday. Not a soul in Concord was baking this morning, I can tell you that."

The soldiers didn't seem to care if the bread was stale. Stacking their deadly bayonets in a corner, they pulled their chairs up, wolfed the food down, and sent back their plates for more. Emily thought how much more human they looked with their hats off, especially Roberts, with his friendly brown eyes.

It was funny how soldiering seemed to be just a job to these men. They'd gotten through this morning's job, the search for weapons, quickly and not very well. The way I rush through home-work before dinner, thought Emily. Now, in-stead of looking for more work, the men were stuffing themselves.

One of the British thumped his pewter mug on the table. "More gin and water, innkeeper."

Mr. Wright gave his cheerful host smile and reached for the square green bottle on the shelf. Then he held it up to the light, squinting. " 'Tis empty, sir. I'll fetch another bottle from the cellar."

The officer looked up from his plate with raised eyebrows. "I noted a full case of gin behind the bar, sir."

Emily, clearing plates, tried not to look concerned. Mr. Wright hesitated just a split second before answering. "Why, yes, sir, a full case of *empty* bottles. I'll go — "

Pushing back his chair, the British officer strolled to the bar. "Empty bottles with corks? Give me one of those bottles, sir."

Mr. Wright had to hand over a bottle, and the officer thumped it on the bar with a leaden rattle. At a gesture from the officer, two of his soldiers picked up the case of musket-ball-filled gin bottles and lugged it outside. Emily and Abigail followed and watched them heave it into the millpond. "Those jerks!" Emily exclaimed.

But Abigail grinned in her innocent-rabbit way. "They're fools not to pour the balls out of the bottles," she reassured Emily. "We'll dredge the pond tomorrow."

Looking around the square, Emily realized the musket balls were not the only loss for the Concord patriots. A couple of redcoats were rolling barrels of flour into the square and smashing them with axes. Some soldiers were tossing barrel staves into a bonfire built with the hacked-up Liberty Pole.

"That fire is far too near the courthouse," said Abigail. "If the breeze shifts, and sparks fly —"

Emily gasped and pointed. A shower of sparks was wafting into the air, sailing up to the courthouse roof. The roof burst into flames like kindling.

As black smoke billowed into the sky, an old woman hobbled out of a house on the square and grabbed at a British officer.

"That's Widow Moulton," said Abigail. "She's begging them to put out the fire. Not likely!"

Emily didn't see why the British would care if the whole village of Concord burned down, either. But the old woman kept begging and pleading, running from officer to officer. Finally one of them gave an impatient command, and soldiers began a bucket chain from the well on the common. The smell of wet charred wood drifted across the square.

Just then, there was a distant *pop-pop-pop* from the direction of the North Bridge. One of the soldiers who had eaten breakfast in the Wright Tavern spoke to the soldier called Roberts. "A skirmish with the Yankee Doodles, eh, Ned?"

"At least they have something to fight for." Ned Roberts spoke absently, staring up the road to the bridge.

Emily gulped. *Were* Matt and Jonathan at the bridge, after all? Where were they when those musket balls, just like the lead balls she'd poured with her own hands, started flying?

A few minutes later, scarlet uniforms appeared around a sharp angle in the road to the bridge. These soldiers were not marching in an orderly way. Some of them were limping, helped along by their comrades. Some of them lay on stretchers with their arms and legs dangling.

A soldier strode down the common, looking right and left at the groups of redcoats. "Ned!" he called. "Where's Ned Roberts gotten to?" he asked a soldier near Emily. "We're to help with the wounded."

Emily stared at the wounded soldiers. She felt cold, as if the April sunshine had stopped pouring down on the common. We shouldn't have come here, she thought. It was my stupid idea to see the American Revolution.

Now there had been a battle. People had been hurt — some of them killed. Where *were* Matt and Jonathan?

7.
The Broken Musket

When the British officer shouted "Halt!" on the moonlit road to Concord, Jonathan dove for the woods. "This is an emergency," he muttered. He zigzagged through the trees like a character in a video game.

"In an emergency," Jonathan explained to himself, "the important thing is not to panic."

Tripping over a log, Jonathan sprawled on a bed of pine needles. He stumbled to his feet.

"Stay calm," he gasped.

He ran a few yards, tripped, and fell again.

Out of breath, Jonathan continued his instructions silently: Keep a relaxed but alert frame of mind, so you can make split-second decisions about —

Glancing over his shoulder, Jonathan caught himself by the neck on a low-hanging pine branch. He clutched the branch and stood there with his heart thudding.

As he calmed down, Jonathan wondered why

he hadn't heard any footsteps from Matt or Emily. He'd thought they were behind him, but maybe they were ahead of him. He'd go a little farther into the woods, out of earshot (and gunshot) of the British, before he tried calling.

Stepping carefully so as not to make twigs crack or leaves crunch, Jonathan picked his way among the trees. After several minutes, he paused and scanned the woods. The dappled moonlight and shadow acted like camouflage. He could imagine a redcoat behind each tree, waiting with pistol cocked to hear Jonathan's voice. On the other hand, Matt and Emily might be behind those same trees.

Afraid to shout, Jonathan walked on. "Stupid," he muttered to himself. "We are really stupid." He was realizing that he'd almost expected to watch the beginning of the Revolution as if he were sitting up on bleachers. The minutemen and the redcoats would act out their parts for him on a playing field.

But of course the three kids from the future *weren't* in the bleachers. They were right in the middle of the action. And they'd walked smack into the British patrol hiding in ambush, like state troopers on a highway. Except that the British sure weren't handing out speeding tickets.

Well, at least Jonathan had escaped. The next thing was to find Matt and Emily. They'd head back to the road, wouldn't they? The road was the *only* place between Lexington and Concord where the kids knew where they were.

So the thing to do was get back to the road, somewhere past the ambush. Unfortunately, Jonathan had zigzagged so well that now he wasn't sure which direction the road was.

Jonathan walked on and on, hoping to come out of the woods and find a farmhouse where he could ask directions. He picked his way around rocks and tangles of brambles and over fallen trees, thinking that the woods couldn't go on forever.

Maybe not forever, but these woods went on for hours, at least. The only open space Jonathan came to was a pond. There he sank up to his ankles in a marshy spot, and almost lost a shoe.

At one point Jonathan heard a deep-voiced bell clanging in the distance. He remembered a couple of lines of Longfellow's poem about the midnight ride of Paul Revere: " . . . spread the alarm/Through every Middlesex village and farm/For the country-folk to be up and to arm."

If he walked toward the sound of the bell, he'd come to a meetinghouse in a village. But if that village weren't Concord or Lexington, he'd be way out of his way.

Not that you're not way out of your way as it is, thought Jonathan wearily. Some incredibly crafty woodsman you are, Schultz. You're the kind of woodsman who needs a paved road and a big green highway sign that says CONCORD, with a pointing arrow. Pathetic.

The fallen trees and boulders and snarls of brambles were beginning to look familiar. He couldn't have been walking in a huge circle this whole time, could he? Wait — there through the trees was a flat moonlit surface.

Was that the road? Jonathan's spirits lifted. He almost charged through the last trees — and caught himself at the edge of a downward slope. The flat surface was a pond. It looked exactly like the pond where he'd stepped in the mud.

It *was* the same pond. He *had* been walking in a big circle.

How could he get so lost? Jonathan felt an anxious tightness in his throat. This wasn't a wilderness. If it weren't nighttime, he was sure he could climb to the top of a hill and spot a farm. So, maybe the only sensible thing to do was stay put and wait until it wasn't nighttime.

Jonathan peered and stumbled around until he found a drift of dry leaves at the base of a broad tree trunk. Settling against the trunk with his knees drawn up, he wrapped his arms around himself. As the cool night air drifted through his shirt, he tried not to think about his cozy sleeping bag on Matt's carpeted bedroom floor, two hundred-plus years in the future.

Cold as he was, Jonathan finally dozed off. He

dreamed that he'd figured out a way to use the
TASC without standing in the picture. He'd
pressed a secret button on the TASC control and
gone back to Matt's bedroom for a time-out
snooze. He was snuggling into his sleeping bag,
feeling guilty about leaving his friends. But
somehow his sleeping bag had been outfitted
with a refrigeration unit, which he couldn't turn
off.

Jonathan woke out of his uncomfortable doze.
The woods were still dark, but now the sky was
definitely blue. Not only that — Jonathan
pushed himself to his feet. The nearby pond
seemed to flow into a pasture — he could just
glimpse it through the trees. He stumbled forward on stiff legs. Yes!

Out of the trees, Jonathan swung his legs over
a low wall and climbed up the slope of the pasture. At the top of the rise he found himself
looking down at an orchard, rows of white-blos-
soming trees. And past the orchard, a barn. And
half-hidden behind the barn, sure enough, a
house.

Jonathan hurried through the orchard. The
windows of the farmhouse were dark, but farmers always got up early, didn't they? Maybe they
just didn't turn on the lights — light candles,
that is.

On the hard-packed dirt around the barn, Jonathan slowed down. This was a working farm, all right — he sniffed the county fair smell of farm animals nearby.

"Git back, ye rascally vagabond!" Someone with a pitchfork, pointed at Jonathan's stomach, lunged out from behind the barn.

Stopping with a gasp, Jonathan put his hands up. He couldn't see his attacker well, silhouetted against the sunrise. But the shoulders were bent, and the voice rasped like an old man's.

Blinking, Jonathan forced a smile. "Hey, relax! I'm not a vagabond. Just a time traveler — just a *traveler*." Whew! He wasn't really awake yet. "Jonathan Schultz, from Newbury-on-Hudson, New York."

The old man lowered his pitchfork, but he didn't put it down. "Humph. A traveling thief, more likely. Thought ye saw your chance, didn't ye, with the able-bodied men called out against the Regulars? Moses Raymond" — he jerked a thumb at himself — "may be stiff in the knees, but — "

"Listen, I'm sorry," said Jonathan earnestly. "Sir. Look, I didn't mean to scare you. I got lost, and I thought you could tell me how to get to Concord."

Peering more closely at Jonathan, Mr. Raymond blew out his breath with a scornful noise. "Who's a-feared? Ye're nothing but a boy, in spite of those feet the size of platters." He leaned on his pitchfork. "Be that as it may, I can see ye're no vagabond. And no country boy, in spite of the leaves in your hair."

Jonathan brushed at his wig and tried to smile again. "You're right, sir. I live in a town."

"Ah." A thoughtful light came into the old man's eyes. "A runaway 'prentice, eh?"

Jonathan had to think for a moment, to figure out what the old man was talking about. "Oh — an apprentice. You mean, like I'm learning a trade by helping someone out in a shop. Well — sort of." He thought of all the afternoons and weekends he'd spent in the garage workshop of Mr. Kenny, Matt's great-grandfather.

It was getting lighter by the minute. Stepping aside so that he wasn't looking into the sun, Jonathan could see Mr. Raymond's weather-beaten face with its shaggy eyebrows. The old farmer's expression was almost friendly.

"Well, now." Mr. Raymond set his pitchfork against the barn wall and jerked his head toward the house. "Likely ye could do with a bite to eat."

Food! Jonathan felt more and more cheerful. As he followed Mr. Raymond's stiff-legged gait across the barnyard, he noticed the moon setting behind the farmhouse chimney. Birds darted across the clear sky. It was a beautiful morning.

At the door of the house, Mr. Raymond gave Jonathan a sharp glance from under his bristly eyebrows. "What kind of 'prentice might ye be?"

"What kind of apprentice?" Jonathan hesitated, thinking again of Mr. Kenny's garage. "I work in a fixit shop — I mean, a shop that repairs all kinds of machines."

Mr. Raymond led Jonathan into the kitchen. "Not a gunsmith's 'prentice, hey?" He sounded disappointed.

Jonathan was beginning to get the drift. "You've got a gun you want fixed?" He followed the old man's gaze to a long gun on the wall.

"She's served me well," said Mr. Raymond, nodding at his musket. "I carried her against the French and Injuns at Lake Champlain. I've brought down many a grouse and turkey with her. But now, just when the redcoats start a-tramping about the country, she's broke." The old man pointed to the empty set of pegs above the musket. "Of course, Caleb, that's my son in the minutemen, he took the new gun. Smuggled out of Boston last year in a cartload of manure, it was, right under the noses of the redcoats." He chortled.

Reaching up, Jonathan lifted the musket off its pegs. "But this one doesn't work? *Whew.*" It was heavier than he expected. And it must have been at least five feet long.

"Aye, she's broke. No time to bring her over to Samuel Hartwell; he's the gunsmith in Lincoln. I'd try to fix her myself, except I can't see close to, nowadays. And my fingers are so stiff." He spread out his gnarled, calloused hands.

Jonathan looked the gun over carefully. He noted the ramrod fitted along the underside of the barrel, the worn, polished wooden stock, the flat little square of flint sticking up where the stock met the barrel. Pointing the barrel at an empty corner, he flexed the trigger. "I think I get it. The flint strikes sparks on this little metal part, and the sparks fall into this little dish part and light the powder . . . so, what isn't working?"

As the old man explained, Jonathan laid the musket on the table, near the window, and began to take it apart. "No problem," he assured Mr. Raymond. "I've fixed all kinds of machines: a toaster, a lawn mower, a time machine — " Whoops!

"A timepiece?" The old man raised his shaggy eyebrows suspiciously. "Don't go a-boasting of fixing clocks, or I won't believe ye can repair a gun."

"No problem," repeated Jonathan, relieved. To Mr. Raymond, "time machine" meant a clock. "This isn't even a real repair — it's a simple matter of . . . " He began to hum, slipping into the trance that came over him when he worked on machines.

The farmhouse didn't have a gunsmith's tools, but Jonathan made do with a knife and a mallet and a couple of odd implements. Before he put the musket back together, he cleaned all the parts and oiled them with a fishy smelling oil that Mr. Raymond brought out.

"There you go." Wiping the musket with a rag, Jonathan looked up to see three people watching him: Mr. Raymond, a woman holding a pail of milk, and a young boy with an armful of kindling.

"Daughter, grandson," said Mr. Raymond to the woman and the boy. "This is Jonathan from New York. He's fixed my musket. He'll break fast with us."

The woman's eyes shone. "Is it not Providence that sent him to us?" she asked the old man. She set a loaf of bread, a knife, and a dish of butter on the kitchen table, and poured milk into four wooden cups. "Do you recall the scripture Reverend Emerson read at Sunday meeting? 'The stranger that dwelleth with you shall be unto you as one born among you.'"

Jonathan turned away, embarrassed, and hung the musket back on the wall. He was beginning to understand what the musket meant to the Raymonds. He could imagine the three of them huddled in the farmhouse, as a band of redcoat looters tramped across their fields. The old farmer would be crouched by the window, his stiff-jointed fingers fumbling with his powder horn and musket as he loaded and shot and had to load before he could shoot again. How good a shot was the old man?

Mr. Raymond said a short blessing over the food, and the four of them sat down at the table. The bread was dense like pumpernickel, without the sour taste. The butter was sweet. Mr. Raymond's daughter kept cutting more bread, and Jonathan kept eating.

After a moment the old man remarked, "My mind's at rest now, with my gun ready." As if in answer to Jonathan's worry, he added, "My aim's not what it used to be, but I guess I can hit a scarlet coat at fifty yards." He gave a grim chuckle.

Remembering how Mr. Kingsley had called the rebelling Colonists "rabble," Jonathan wished the Britisher could meet the Raymonds. *Rabble* — as if these hardworking farm people had nothing better to do than stir up trouble! Even Mr. Kingsley would have to see that they were fighting to defend their homes and their families.

Jonathan munched a couple more slices of the hearty bread. The woman refilled his cup with milk. Full at last, Jonathan realized he'd better be on his way.

It must be seven o'clock, at least. There was going to be that famous battle at the North

Bridge in Concord, sometime this morning. "So, Mr. Raymond, could you tell me how to get to Concord?"

"Concord," repeated the woman. "The patriots in Concord were wanting a gunsmith, were they not, Father?"

"Aye." The old man explained to Jonathan the way to the village of Concord. Then he tapped Jonathan's arm with a gnarled finger. "When ye get to Concord center, go straight to the blacksmith. He's been a-making musket barrels in his shop. Now, tell him that Moses Raymond sent ye because ye fixed his musket." He nodded and patted Jonathan's arm. "I'd be surprised if he didn't have work for ye."

"Thank you very much, sir," said Jonathan. These were really nice people. If he *had* been a runaway apprentice, he'd be delighted to get a job like that. "How far is it from here to Concord?"

"To the village center, some two-and-a-half miles," answered the woman.

Jonathan swallowed the last of his milk and stood up. Two and a half miles would be nothing on his bike, or even on his skateboard. But he had to walk. And he'd better get there soon, so he could look around for Matt and Emily before the battle.

8.
A Fire in Concord

After hasty thanks and good-byes at the Raymonds' doorstep, Jonathan loped past the barn in long-legged strides. He jogged up the slope through the orchard, breathing in the scent of apple blossoms. On the other side of the rise, in the walled pasture, cows were now grazing. At the far end of the pasture, a pond reflected the blue sky.

As Mr. Raymond had advised him, Jonathan took the cart track around the pond. He crossed a brook and found what he thought was the right path into a patch of maple woods. But once he was surrounded by trees, he paused again.

What exactly had Mr. Raymond meant by his next direction, "Where the woods are middling thick"? Jonathan didn't want to start wandering in circles, the way he had the night before.

As Jonathan hesitated, twigs cracked on the path behind him. Through the bare-branched trees and undergrowth appeared a man with a musket. There was only one reason, Jonathan guessed, why a man with a gun would be running through the countryside today.

"Hey, excuse me!" called Jonathan as the man came closer. "If you're going to Concord, do you mind if I — "

"Stand aside!" barked the man. He was young, no more than twenty, with a long jaw and a freckled nose. "The Regulars are out. I'm joining the minutemen."

Jonathan jumped out of his way, but only to run after him. "I won't bother you," he panted. "It's just that I don't know the way to Concord."

The other trotted on through the woods without turning or answering, which Jonathan took as permission to follow. It wasn't easy to keep up; the heavy musket didn't seem to slow the young man at all.

Finally they reached the edge of the woods. The youth paused, wiping sweat from his forehead with his shirtsleeve. He turned to frown at Jonathan. "It may come to fighting, in Concord. Why aren't you home, helping your mother with the livestock?"

Jonathan gave a startled laugh at this idea of his mother, who wouldn't even touch his pet iguana. But before he could answer, the young man looked him up and down and smiled. "Nay, what am I saying? You're not from these parts."

Under the Colonial youth's stare, Jonathan

was suddenly aware that everything he had on, from his loafers to his wig, was factory-made. And everything the young minuteman wore, from the thong tying back his blond hair to his knit stockings, looked made by hand.

"Yeah, I'm from New York." Jonathan fell into step with the young farmer as they walked on. He hoped "New York" would explain it all, including the bunchy hemming job Emily had done on his cutoff sweatpants. "Jonathan Schultz."

The young man nodded and jerked a thumb at himself. "Amos Loring." As they tramped over the fields, Amos explained what Jonathan already knew, that the British had marched out from Boston to seize the Colonists' military stores at Concord.

"Father's already with the minutemen," Amos went on. "He left for the village at the first alarm, last night. I had to stay home to get the livestock settled. You might think I could be spared, with four younger brothers, but Father says they still need watching."

"Five kids in your family, huh?" asked Jonathan. That seemed like a lot.

"Nine," corrected Amos. "Four sisters, not counting baby Sara — she died from the summer sickness two years back. Well, they'll have to get along without me, after this year's harvest."

"You mean, because you'll be in the army?" asked Jonathan.

Amos looked puzzled. "What army? No, I mean I'm going out west. Now that Ezra's turning sixteen this year, Father says I can leave and homestead a farm of my own. There's still good land to be had in Vermont."

As Jonathan thought over the idea of Vermont as "out west," Amos turned and shaded his eyes to glance at the sun. It had risen well above the hills. "Too much talk." Gripping his musket more firmly, he broke into a trot again. Jonathan trotted after him, stumbling over rocks and clumps of grass.

A short while later, Amos paused at the foot of a boulder-dotted slope. "Hear that?" There was an eager half-smile on his face as he listened to the shrill piping and the steady rattle. "It's our fife and drum. We're marching out to meet the redcoats!"

They scrambled over the rise, and a broad dirt road came into view. A column of men dressed like Amos were disappearing around a bend.

"Stay out of sight, Jonathan!" Amos pointed to the ridge rising from the other side of the road. Plunging down the slope, he pounded along the road after his fellow minutemen. His powder horn bumped his hip as he ran.

Jonathan's heart had started tripping in time to the brisk beat of the drum. Crossing the road, he found himself thinking, Maybe I could go see the blacksmith, like Mr. Raymond said. Help them make guns for a while. I could help them win the Revolution.

Shocked at his own thoughts, Jonathan put an anxious hand on the pouch tied to his belt. He pressed the flat shape of the TASC control, his lifeline to his own time. You're only visiting here, he reminded himself.

On the other side of the road, Jonathan climbed the ridge as Amos had advised. Shading his eyes from the morning sun, he spotted the straggly column of gray and dark blue and brown. The Colonial forces, marching east. There must have been about two hundred of them.

And then, farther down the road and headed straight toward them, a bright red column snaked into view. The white breeches on the redcoats' legs moved precisely together, *one,* two, *one,* two. From this distance, the British column looked like one monster creature, a scarlet centipede.

There were a lot more of the British — three times as many, Jonathan guessed. Coming right at Amos and his father and Mr. Raymond's son and all their relatives and friends and neighbors. He held his breath.

Then the gray and brown column stopped. They did a sloppy about-face. The fife player and the drummer pushed forward to the new head of the column, and the minutemen began to march back toward Concord.

When the minutemen had almost reached the part of the road below Jonathan, he realized that the same jaunty fife-and-drum music was coming from two different places. The British fifes were tweetling the same tune as the Colonists, and the British drums were beating out the same rhythm. Some of the Colonists were grinning, glancing back, as if they were pleased to be in such a fine parade.

How can they fool around like this? Jonathan wondered. Don't they know they're going to kill each other? He'd watched *chess* tournaments where the opponents acted more like enemies.

Hiking along the ridge toward Concord, Jonathan noticed he wasn't the only one up here. More and more colonists with muskets appeared among the trees and rocks. They must be latecomers, like Amos. And now the Concord minutemen were leaving the road, climbing up to join them. Jonathan caught sight of Amos Loring beside an older man in a wide-brimmed farmer's hat. The older man — his father, guessed Jonathan — looked just like Amos, only with a more weathered face and grayed hair.

When all the minutemen were off the road, a man in a three-cornered hat climbed onto a boulder. He squinted into the sun, down the road toward the long red centipede of British troops. Then he turned to the crowd clambering over the hillside. "Fellow soldiers!" he called out.

"Hush," the men told each other. "Heed Major Buttrick."

"To the Liberty Pole!" shouted the major. He swung his arm in the direction of Concord.

The village wasn't far now. Jonathan caught sight of a long pond in a cluster of buildings. The ridge followed the road all the way to the common, then ended in a steep hill above the village.

Reaching the hill, the minutemen gathered around the flagpole. Jonathan, like the others, kept his eyes on the road below, where the British column would come marching into the village.

"The Regulars are climbing the ridge!" came a call from higher up the hill. Sure enough, scarlet dots were now crawling among the rocks and bushes.

"We'll give them a hearty welcome," growled a familiar voice behind Jonathan. He turned to see Amos shaking his musket toward the redcoats.

Major Buttrick called out from under the Liberty Pole. "Forward, toward the North Bridge!"

Amos's father put a hand on the muzzle of his gun. "Not so eager, son. We aren't to fire, unless they fire on us. If you'd been through the French and Indian Wars, you wouldn't be so eager to waste good powder. Major Buttrick" — he nodded toward the leader at the flagpole — "has the right idea. If they head for Barrett's, where the arms are stored, *then* we'll give them a fight."

"Oh, they'll head for Barrett's, never fear," another man spoke up. "A falsehearted Tory spy has told them where the stores are hid. Colonel Barrett rode back earlier, to bury the arms in his fields."

As they talked, they climbed among the headstones, down the side of the hill overlooking the village. The minutemen filtered through a wooded stretch, then up another hill near a river. "There's the Reverend Emerson's parsonage," remarked Amos to Jonathan, pointing down to a house almost on the bank of the river. "See, just before the North Bridge."

"That's the North Bridge?" Jonathan stared. The famous bridge was a little wooden thing, not even as big as a bridge over Interstate 95.

Amos's father had turned to look back at the hill above the village. "That's likely Colonel Smith, the redcoats' commander," he remarked. He pointed at two British on the hilltop, one of them peering through a spyglass. "They say he's a fine porker!"

The men around him laughed. Even from this distance, Jonathan could see that Colonel Smith was twice as fat as the other officer.

Amid the general hum of talk, Jonathan became aware of an argument going on behind him. It was Major Buttrick and a few others, including a man with a thin, intense face under a powdered wig. "That's the Reverend Emerson himself," explained Amos to Jonathan.

It was surprising, thought Jonathan, how involved the ministers were in the fight for freedom. First Reverend Clarke in Lexington, hiding the rebel leaders Hancock and Adams right in his house. Now Reverend Emerson, as eager to blast the British as Amos was.

"Let us stand our ground!" Reverend Emerson had the carrying voice of someone used to public speaking. "If we die, let us die here."

"Discretion is the better part of valor, Reverend Emerson," said Buttrick mildly. "Our numbers increase by the minute, as the militia from other towns join us." He waved a hand around the open countryside. It was true. Colonists were still streaming toward Concord from all directions.

The group of leaders strolled out of earshot, still arguing. But a few minutes later Major Buttrick shouted an order, repeated over the hillside: "Across the bridge!"

On the other side of the river, the motley Colonial troops gathered on the next hill. Jonathan milled around with them, feeling more and more antsy. In the shifting crowd he kept thinking he'd caught sight of Matt or Emily, but he was wrong each time. They weren't there.

Finally Jonathan sat down on a boulder with Amos and his father. He couldn't imagine Matt or Emily missing this historic moment at the North Bridge, if they could possibly help it. Matt especially, the history buff, would show up at the North Bridge if it killed him.

If Jonathan couldn't find Matt and Emily sooner or later, what would he do? He couldn't picture returning to their time and explaining things to his friends' parents. ("Hey, Mr. and Mrs. Cowen, I'm sorry, but these things can happen when you time travel, you know?")

No. He'd have to stay here and become a real gunsmith's apprentice.

Jonathan was drawn out of his worries by a murmur running through the crowd. He stood up and looked around the hillside. There must have been another hundred men on the grassy slope now.

Then Jonathan noticed what everyone else was looking at: the British soldiers marching down the road to the bridge and filing across in rows of four. "Now he's sending half of them up the road," said Amos's father, "to search Barrett's, I'll wager." That detachment disappeared over a hill.

At this distance, thought Jonathan, the scarlet-coated British with the white X's of straps across their chests looked like toy soldiers. He'd played with a set of soldiers like that when he was little.

There were fewer than a hundred of the British left at the bridge. After they spread out along the road, another long time went by. Many of the Colonists on the hill sat down, and some of them got out food to eat. Amos's father shared his bread and cheese with Amos and Jonathan.

Then another wave of murmurs ran over the hill. They all stood up and gazed toward the village, the cluster of buildings beside the long pond. A column of black smoke rose into the sky from the village square.

"The foul redcoats!" exclaimed Amos. "They're burning our houses!"

Just down the slope from Jonathan, Major Buttrick and the other leaders were also staring toward the village. Buttrick stood silent, arms folded. But a solid-built man in a brown suit spoke out so that everyone on the hill could hear.

"The British boast that they can lay waste our villages, and we will not oppose them. And I, Joseph Hosmer, begin to think it is true." A ripple of muttering, "Aye, aye," rose from the crowd. Hosmer swung his arm toward the smoke rising from the center of Concord. "Will you let them burn the town down?"

"No!" The shout burst out of all their throats, including Major Buttrick's — including Jonathan's.

The men scrambled to assemble into units and load their muskets. Amos tipped powder from his palm into the muzzle of his gun and rammed the ball down.

Nobody except Jonathan seemed to notice an extra musket lying on the ground. *Extra?* There weren't any "extra" muskets here. Someone — a deserter — must have sneaked off and left it.

The fife and drum began to play a brisk tune. The troop of Colonists marched down the slope. Jonathan's heart felt as if it were beating in his throat. Hoisting the musket to his shoulder, he staggered after them.

On the road below, the British watched the Colonists for a moment. Then the redcoats hurried back to the bridge. The British soldiers seemed confused, no longer the perfectly coordinated scarlet centipede that had marched into Concord.

Marching at the rear of the ranks of minutemen, Jonathan watched the arch of the wooden bridge loom closer. The redcoats, who had been trying to tear up the planks of the bridge, stopped what they were doing and crowded onto the far end.

Ka-pow, ka-pow.

Jonathan gasped at the shots, flinching as if

he'd been hit. Then he saw the splashes in the river — the British had fired warning shots. A breeze pulled wisps of musket smoke downstream.

The drum beat steadily. The men in brown and gray closed the distance to the bridge. Jonathan, at the heels of the last unit, wondered if his gun was loaded.

The front line of British soldiers raised their muskets. A spatter of gunshots tore the air.

At the head of the Colonial Army's column, two men crumpled and fell. The fife music broke off.

Major Buttrick raised his arms. "Fire, fellow soldiers! For God's sake, fire!"

Muskets went off in a volley, and then another volley. Redcoats fell. Through a blur of blue smoke Jonathan saw the soldiers in red stumbling back, off the bridge. They hesitated in the road, getting in each other's way. Then the British began running back toward the village.

Jonathan's knees were shaking, and suddenly he could hardly hold up his heavy musket. He set the stock on the ground and leaned on the musket, which had not been loaded after all.

The Colonials had won, but Jonathan didn't feel like cheering. Who was lying on the dirt road in front of the bridge? Amos, who had plans to homestead out west this fall? His father, with eight more kids to bring up? At least one red-coated figure — not a toy soldier — was sprawled on the ground.

The musket shots still ringing in Jonathan's ears seemed to echo the crack of the pistol the night before, when they'd stumbled on the British patrol. That pistol was shot harmlessly into the treetops — wasn't it?

Matt would show up at the North Bridge if it killed him. Maybe Jonathan hadn't found Matt because — because his friend was lying somewhere along the road between Lexington and Concord.

9.
A British Son
of Liberty

Standing in front of the Wright Tavern,
Emily watched the British troops straggle
back into the village of Concord from the North
Bridge. She didn't want to listen to the wounded
men groaning, or look at the limp, blood-
smeared bodies on stretchers. But she couldn't
turn away.

Emily glanced at Abigail. The older girl was
biting her lip. "They are the enemy, after all,"
she told Emily, but she looked sorry.

Behind Abigail's shoulder, Mr. Wright's jolly
innkeeper face had gone serious. " 'Tis a cruel
matter," he murmured. Then he noticed Emily
watching him, and he clapped his hands, all
business again. "Abigail, Ethan — look sharp.
We'll have another full tavern before you can
say 'lobsterback.' "

"But I can't stay," whispered Emily as she and
Abigail followed Mr. Wright into the tavern.
Emily had just been stunned by a new thought:

Maybe Matt and Jonathan had never even tried to go to Concord.

Her responsible big brother had probably decided the night before, when they were shot at by the British patrol, that this adventure was too dangerous. He and Jonathan had probably gone straight back to the graveyard in Lexington to wait for her. She had to get out of there.

In the kitchen, Emily started to untie her apron. "Now I really do have to go meet my brother."

"Nay, Ethan!" Looking alarmed, Abigail grabbed Emily's hand. " 'Tisn't wise to go just yet. The British will be leaving Concord soon. You'll be far safer behind them than ahead of them — can't you see that?"

Emily supposed she did, although she also thought Abigail wanted her to stay and help with the tavern work. The two of them barely had time to wipe the tables and sweep the floor before the next customers appeared, just as Mr. Wright had predicted. They were British officers, clomping in the door with their polished black boots.

"This will do for our headquarters," announced an elegantly handsome man with large, dark eyes. He settled himself at a table near the bar, pulling his ruffled lace shirt cuffs neatly down from his scarlet coat sleeves. "Brandy and water, Innkeeper."

"Just as you wish, Major." Taking more orders for drinks and lunch, Mr. Wright seemed delighted to have his tavern full of the enemy for the second time that morning. But Emily thought the soldiers who had searched the tavern this morning had been a lot nicer, especially the one called Ned.

As Emily served the officers plates of stew, she listened to them discussing what had gone wrong. "The expedition has been a farce from the outset," complained one man. "The three-hour delay in the Cambridge marsh! Our intention was to arrive in Concord before daybreak, to seize the arms before the Colonials had time to gather."

"And consider what occurred just now," another officer put in. "When the captain sent to Colonel Smith for reinforcements at the North Bridge, the colonel took half an hour to waddle a quarter mile! Naturally the battle was lost before he was halfway to the bridge."

"Nevertheless." The major at the table near the bar did not speak loudly, but the others stopped talking. "Nevertheless, gentlemen," he went on, "we are the king's men. We, not the rebels, have the trained and disciplined forces."

The door of the tavern opened, and the bulk of Colonel Smith's red coat filled the door. The other officers rose to their feet. "Sit down, Major Pitcairn," said Smith to the handsome officer.

"At ease, all." He took a chair at Pitcairn's table, and the tavern keeper quickly set a glass in front of him.

Pitcairn smiled. He stirred his own brandy and water with his forefinger and sucked it in a refined manner. "I was about to say, sir: I intend to stir the Yankee blood so, before night."

The officers laughed and raised their glasses. Emily stared at them, wanting to knock their drinks into their faces. She glanced at Mr. Wright. He must have heard, but he kept on filling more glasses at the bar, as if his main concern with these enemy officers was adding up their tabs.

When Emily reported Major Pitcairn's speech in the kitchen, Abigail shrugged. "Let the redcoats boast. They've marched all the way from Boston to seize a few sorry musket balls. And now they've been soundly beaten at the North Bridge, and they must return to Boston."

"How do you know when they'll leave?" asked Emily. "They might decide to stay overnight."

But Abigail was sure they wouldn't. Mr. Wright, stepping into the kitchen to see how much food was left, agreed. "They cannot tarry. They can see for themselves that the minutemen are gathering from all over Massachusetts. If the British remain — " He brought his hands toward each other and made a twisting motion, as if he were wringing a chicken's neck.

But Colonel Smith didn't seem to understand the danger. The British didn't leave, and they didn't leave. From his table in the Wright Tavern, Smith gave leisurely orders about the care of the wounded and finding carriages to cart them back to Boston. He also ordered his troops to march up and down the village, "to inspire fear in the Colonials until we are joined by Lord Percy's reinforcements." Emily saw two of the younger officers exchange glances, as if they thought this was stupid.

Emily had decided by now that Abigail had been trying to scare her into staying at the tavern and working. She looked for a chance to sneak away, but Mr. Wright and Abigail seemed to be taking turns keeping an eye on her.

The only good thing about staying at the tavern was that Emily got to have lunch. After all the officers had eaten, and then Mr. Wright, and then Abigail, Emily was allowed to sit down in the kitchen with a plate of stew. She gobbled it up, including some vegetables — turnips? — that she never would have touched at home.

Finally, as the grandfather clock in Mr. Wright's parlor struck eleven-thirty, Colonel Smith gave his troops orders to prepare to leave. Mr. Wright and Abigail stepped outside to watch the bright red ranks line up on the common, between the tavern and the steep hill where the Liberty Pole had stood. Emily started to step out beside Abigail. Then, realizing this was her chance, she tiptoed back through the taproom and the kitchen.

Dropping her apron on a bench, Emily slipped out the back door. It was too bad not to say good-bye to Abigail and Mr. Wright, but she was afraid they'd try to make her stay.

Emily left Concord the way she'd come in, by the road over the mill dam. Then she turned and walked along the grassy edge of the mill pond, which became the mill brook. The brook seemed to run in the same direction as the road between Concord and Lexington. So if she followed the brook upstream, Emily reasoned, she'd be heading for Lexington but keeping clear of the British.

Glad to be outside again, Emily breathed in the freshwater smell of the brook. It would have been a great day for a walk, if she hadn't been up all night and then on her feet for the last few hours.

Sunshine glinted off the brook into Emily's eyes, dazzling her; sunshine soaked into the top of her head and seemed to soften her brain. She walked on and on, following the twisting and turning of the brook through marshy meadows. The brook forked, and she took the near fork for no particular reason.

Finally, as the brook took a definite turn in another direction, Emily stopped and shook her head. She had no idea where she was, or where the road to Lexington was. Or how to get from here to there.

Some distance ahead of her, where the land began to rise from the meadows, there was a red barn and farmhouse. It was time to ask directions.

But as Emily came closer to the house, she could see that the windows were shuttered. Maybe these people, like the Hartwells, had left for fear of the British. Or maybe the owners of the house were inside, keeping quiet in case the British came by.

Emily thought she heard a noise inside, like footsteps. She knocked on the farmhouse door. When there was no answer, she lifted the latch and stuck her head in.

With the windows shuttered, it was dark inside the house. There was a lingering smell of fried bacon. If these people had gone, they couldn't have left very long ago.

Sunlight from the open door fell across the floorboards and the foot of the stairs. To the right, an open door led to another room. Emily's eyes, used to the sunshine, could barely make out a four-poster bed and —

Emily gasped. With a flash of a white shirt and a gleam from a bayonet, a tall man popped out from behind the bedroom door. Emily screamed and jumped backward.

Then the man lowered his bayonet. The fierce glare in his little brown eyes turned to amusement. "It's the lad from the tavern!"

Emily, stumbling on the doorstep, focused on the man's face. "Ned Roberts?" Her heart was beating fast. "But what are you doing *here*?" She glanced past Ned into the bedroom. His bright red coat was on the floor beside an open chest.

Looking back at the British soldier, Emily noticed the leather breeches he was wearing in place of his uniform pants. "Why did you change — oh."

Watching her as if he wanted to read her mind, Ned spoke in a tight voice. "There you have it. I'm deserting. What's more, I'm thieving."

"No," said Emily. Now it made sense to her, what she'd overheard Ned say in Concord: "At least they have something to fight for."

"This is *not* like stealing," Emily went on. "When the people who live here find your uniform, they'll know why you needed the clothes."

Ned's face relaxed a little, but he shrugged as if he wasn't sure how understanding this farmer would be. "To be sure, my uniform is worth something. The brass buttons and buckles alone would fetch a few shillings."

While Ned went back to rummaging in the chest, Emily closed the front door and kept watch through a crack in the shutter. Then it struck her that someone might come up to the house from the back, so she went through to the kitchen and peered out in that direction. But the sunny fields were empty, except for a flock of crows.

Returning to the foot of the stairs, Emily glanced into the other room. Ned was pulling a homespun shirt over his head, his back to her. His skin was crisscrossed with long white scars.

"Ned!" she exclaimed. "Were you almost killed in a battle, or something?"

His head popping out of the farmer's shirt, Ned turned with a puzzled face. "Battle? I've never been badly wounded. Oh — I take your meaning." One hand went to his back, and his mouth twisted in a grim smile. "Those souvenirs of my service to the king. Twenty lashes for the least offense."

Emily's throat tightened with anger. "They *whipped* you in the army? That's like you were a prisoner."

Ned lifted a gray coat from the chest and held it up to his shoulders, frowning. "A bit small for me, but it'll have to do." As he tugged on the coat, he looked straight into Emily's eyes. "Aye. There you have it. A prisoner. Now I want my liberty, same as your minutemen are fighting for."

Thinking about what the British army would do to a deserter, Emily was anxious for Ned to get away. But he insisted on leaving a note. They couldn't find any paper or ink in the house, so Ned took a piece of charcoal from the bedroom fireplace and scrawled a few words on the wall:

Sir: I am forever in your Debt.

"I don't think you should sign your real name," said Emily quickly.

Nodding, Ned thought a moment, then wrote again:

A British Son of Liberty

Outside the farmhouse, Ned paused at the well to dunk his head in a bucket and wash the powder out of his hair. As he came up dripping, Emily gave him a big grin. "Now you look just like a patriot!"

Grinning back, Ned retied his wet brown hair. He clapped her on the shoulder. "Fare well, lad." He turned his head toward shots in the distance. "They're fighting on the Lexington road." He pointed past the barn, to fields backed by a thin line of woods. "Stay clear of the Regulars. They're in a foul temper, likely to fire at anything that moves. They'd pick you off like a rabbit."

10.
The Battle Road

Shouldering his musket, Ned headed off across a pasture. Emily hurried in the opposite direction, the way Ned had pointed toward the road. When she turned a few moments later, she could barely make out Ned's figure on the other side of a clump of trees. His farmer's clothes blended into the dull colors of the bare trees and underbrush.

In spite of Abigail's and Ned's warnings, Emily hoped she could beat the British troops to the road. It seemed like a good idea for the three kids from the future to *leave* before the next battle caught up with them. And the battle seemed to be flowing toward Lexington.

Now Emily could see the road, maybe the length of a playing field away through the sparse woods. Over the now-and-then cracks of musket fire, she heard a steady shuffling, creaking noise. At first she didn't know what it was, because it sounded so different from the crisp *tramp, tramp, tramp* of the British troops marching past the Hartwells' this morning.

It was too late to reach the road before the British. Emily paused among the trees to watch the redcoats' column round the curve of the road. Several of the soldiers were hobbling or limping. The creaking came from the wheels of wagons — the wagons Colonel Smith had ordered for the wounded who couldn't even limp.

Staring at the British retreat, Emily barely noticed a British soldier raising his musket and pointing toward the woods. In the last split second, she realized he was aiming at her.

Ka-pow! Something whistled over her head. Emily found herself on her knees behind a tree, her heart tripping. It wasn't a very big tree. She tried to make herself fit exactly behind the trunk.

Ka-pow! That second shot had come from off to her left, where Colonists were darting through the trees.

There was a scream from the road. One of the British bawled, "Stand and fight, you cowardly concealed villains!"

Still crouched behind her skimpy shelter, Emily watched minutemen running hunched over from tree to tree. One of them called, "Get away from the road, boy!" Another shouted, "Sit tight till they're past!"

Emily paid no attention to either piece of advice. There was a humming in her head. Somehow the gunfire and the shouting and running around her were lifting her to another level of energy. She couldn't stay still. Like a runner stealing third base, she darted out from behind her tree and zigzagged after the minutemen.

The ground sloped upward, and the trees thinned out. Emily paused behind a boulder, panting. Between her and the road, five or six minutemen knelt behind a stone wall. They fired over the wall at the straggling column of redcoats, then dropped out of sight to reload their muskets. Gunsmoke floated over the slope, making Emily cough.

A British officer shouted an order. Redcoats broke away from the column and charged off the road with bayonets ready. Emily tensed to dash out from behind her boulder.

Then something farther up the hill caught her eye. It was a minuteman running the wrong way. A small, young minuteman with odd hair. He was trying to take cover like the others, but he stooped behind a bush without seeming to notice the British soldier circling behind him.

"Matt!" screamed Emily.

At the sound of her voice, Matt jumped up, staring around. The redcoat took aim.

Ka-pow!

The British soldier slumped, dropping his gun. A minuteman with a smoking musket ran past. "Move on!" he shouted at Matt. "They're flanking."

Her heart pounding so hard she felt sick, Emily darted forward to Matt's bush. She grabbed his arm and yanked him up. Without speaking, they sprinted away from the road, around the hill, until they were out of sight of the battleground.

Matt plopped down on a boulder, his face red and sweaty. Emily sat beside him. He didn't say anything about almost getting shot. Emily didn't want to talk about it, either. She handed him her handkerchief, and he wiped his face and neck.

Finally Emily spoke. "Where's Jonathan?"

Matt nodded in the direction of Lexington. "Waiting in the graveyard, in case I missed you on the road." He gave his sister a grim look. "When you didn't show up with Jonathan, I thought — I had to come and see if you got shot by the patrol last night."

"But this is *way* past where the patrol was," argued Emily. She could tell Matt had been worried sick about her. But she didn't want to think about what had almost happened because he'd come looking for her.

"I wouldn't know, because I only got as far as the patrol." Matt told her about being captured and meeting Paul Revere.

"You're lucky!" exclaimed Emily. She told him

about baby-sitting for the Hartwells. "But I did get to ride this excellent horse."

Matt seemed to pull himself together, letting out a long sigh. "Hey, we can talk on the way back to Lexington. Jonathan's waiting. The battle must have moved on down the road, by now."

Cautiously Matt and Emily crept back around the hill. They didn't want to take the chance of actually walking on the road, but they kept it in sight so they could follow it. Here and there Emily caught sight of a man in a scarlet uniform sprawled by the way, not moving. She couldn't help wondering if any of them were the soldiers she'd served that morning.

Emily and Matt climbed up one side of a hill and down the other. They passed in back of a shuttered tavern. Meanwhile, Matt told her all about Paul Revere. He told her about the battle on the Lexington common at dawn, and about how he almost got blown up.

"Then all of a sudden, the British officers got their soldiers calmed down," said Matt. "And they just gave three cheers for their big victory and marched out of town."

They clambered across a ravine with a stream at the bottom. The way to Lexington was beginning to seem like an obstacle course, thought Emily. "So, did you even think about going to Concord? Or did you go straight to the graveyard and wait there the whole time?"

"I *thought* about going to Concord, to the North Bridge," admitted Matt. "But there was so much to do in Lexington, I couldn't just say, 'Excuse me, I've got to go see another battle.' People would tell me to do something, and I'd do it. They'd tell me to fetch water, and I'd go fetch water. They'd tell me to get cloth for bandages, and I'd get it. I gave someone my handkerchief for a bandage. Every so often, I'd run to the graveyard to see if there was any sign of you or Jonathan."

"Then you probably realized it was too late for the North Bridge," said Emily.

"Right, because I knew that battle was in the morning," agreed Matt. *"Then* Reverend Clarke got hold of me." He grinned. "Remember the big guy in the doorway at the parsonage? That was Reverend Clarke. Before I knew it, I was helping him hide his money and silver and stuff. We put some under the potatoes in the cellar and some in the attic."

"But why was he hiding his things *after* the British came through Lexington?" asked Emily. She stumbled over a plowed field, noticing a dark brown farmhouse on the other side of the road. "Hey, that's the Hartwells'. The British didn't burn their house, after all."

"Because Reverend Clarke knew the British had to go *back* to Boston through Lexington," Matt answered her question. "And by that time they'd probably be mad and feel like looting. Anyway, then there was a funeral for the guys who were killed on the common this morning." He trudged along silently for a moment, staring at the furrows. "I helped cut pine branches to cover the graves."

Emily was silent, too. She wondered what had happened to Samuel Hartwell, patriot, husband of Mary, father of Polly, Sally, and baby Lucy.

Matt and Emily plodded on, past a few more farms. "I wish I were riding Dancer," sighed Emily. "I'm getting a blister on my heel from these moccasins."

Her brother gave her a tired grin. "Massachusetts looks so little on the map. But it sure isn't little when you try to walk around in it. You know — I bet it's safe to walk on the road now."

Emily followed her brother down to the road without any discussion. Even a rutted dirt road was a pleasure to walk on, after clambering over the countryside. "So, when did Jonathan show up?" she asked.

"Not until a little while ago," answered Matt, "because he went all the way to the North Bridge. Then when he didn't see us, he decided to come back this way and look for us. But before he left Concord, one of the minutemen leaders found out he's a gunsmith's apprentice."

"What do you mean, 'found out'?" Emily started to laugh.

Matt smiled and shrugged. "You know Jonathan. He lands in 1775, and the next thing you know, he's fixing someone's musket. Anyway, Captain Somebody took him off and had a long discussion about guns with him and fed him lunch. I'm not kidding, I think Jonathan was almost tempted to stay there and join them."

"I know," murmured Emily.

There was a thoughtful silence. Then Matt remarked, "Don't you think it's kind of funny how we feel it's *our* Revolution?"

"Of course we do," said Emily. "We're Americans."

"Yeah, but nobody in our family was here in 1775," said Matt. "Jonathan and I were talking about this. The Cowens came to America in the early 1900s. And Jonathan's people, the Schultzes, came over in the late 1800s — they were German pioneers. But it's as if the people who fought the Revolution were fighting for us, too."

Emily and Matt passed another farmhouse and trudged up a long hill. In the distance, gunfire popped.

"Here we are," said Matt.

They were at the top of the rise, looking down at the village of Lexington. There was the triangular common with the meetinghouse at the top and the tavern to the side. And there was the battle they'd been following.

On the near side of the common, minutemen clustered in small groups behind houses, in back of stone walls, in patches of trees. Farther up the common, a crowd of redcoats scrambled and stumbled past the meetinghouse like red ants. Shots from the minutemen rang out, but the British didn't even stop to fire back.

As the minutemen sneaked after the enemy, keeping behind cover, Emily noticed another splotch of red on the scene. Down the road past the meetinghouse, more British were drawn up in neat ranks. The last of the redcoats from Concord straggled off the common and through the lines of their rescuers.

Ka-boom. There was a splintering crash. A hole appeared in the back wall of the meetinghouse.

"The British reinforcements have a cannon!" Matt pointed to the puff of white smoke rising from a hill beyond Lexington.

The minutemen around the common drew back out of sight. Far as she was from the battle, Emily felt like hiding from the cannon, herself. Somehow one cannon was ten times as frightening as all those hundreds of muskets. Matt looked pale, as if he thought so, too.

"What happens next?" asked Emily in a small voice.

Matt shrugged and shook his head. "I don't really know. That's the trouble with that book you got from the library — the pictures are great, but the history kind of jumps from one thing to another. That's why I didn't know Paul Revere was going to get captured."

It seemed to Emily that her brother was trying to blame her for getting the wrong book, but she let it go. "Anyway, we'd better get down to the graveyard."

Starting down the hill, Emily tried not to think that they were heading *toward* the cannon. She began to trot, then run, and Matt kept pace. The sooner they got to the graveyard and lined up between the headstones and Jonathan pressed the TRANSPORT button, the better.

But as they cut across the fields toward the low wall around the burying ground, Emily forgot about the cannon. "Where's Jonathan?" she panted. Her eyes searched the rows of headstones.

"Schultz," groaned Matt.

A sick, cold feeling came over Emily. Someone was lying facedown at the foot of the far wall. A long, skinny someone.

11.
George Kingsley Doesn't Get It

No! Emily pushed the thought back before she could even think it. She and Matt plunged across the last stretch of ground as if they were racing.

Vaulting the wall at the same moment, Emily and Matt stumbled toward the body on the other side of the graveyard. "Schultz!" Matt almost screamed.

The body raised his narrow face. He scrambled to his hands and knees. "What took you so long?"

Dropping to her knees beside him, Emily gave him a fierce hug. "Jonathan! I thought you were — " He felt awkward and bony, but he sort of hugged her back.

Matt grinned shakily and punched his friend in the arm. "What were you lying on the ground for, you doofus?"

Jonathan gave him an indignant stare. "Like,

because there's a battle going on? Because they just fired a cannon in this direction?"

Emily stiffened, staring toward the common. Beyond the buildings and trees, she could see the top of the hill where the British had set up their artillery.

Without any discussion, the three kids edged closer to the wall. Emily let out a long sigh. Then, looking from Jonathan to Matt, she began to giggle. "You guys should see yourselves."

Matt's variety-store wig was half pulled out of the ribbon in back, the hair sticking up every which way. His white shirt — *Mom's* white shirt — was smeared with dirt and soot. So was his face. Jonathan was just as dirty. His right shoe and sock were gray with dried mud, and his black wig was tucked into his belt like a scalp.

"Yeah, we're a mess," said Jonathan. "But you look gorgeous. What's your secret?"

Glancing down at herself, Emily noticed spatters of stew on her shirtsleeves, and horse sweat on her knee pants, and just plain dirt on her knees and elbows.

Ka-boom.

All three of them dropped flat behind the wall. "Let's get out of here," gasped Matt.

"No argument. Let me get the TASC control." Jonathan rolled over on his side to untie the leather pouch at his belt. "But where do we fit in? The burying ground looks different."

Emily's stomach tightened as she gazed around the graveyard. It looked different to her, too. Of course it was broad daylight now, not moonlight. And they were probably facing a different direction. "I don't remember those piles of pine branches. . . . Oh." Matt had told her about the funeral, about cutting branches to cover the new graves.

"Come on!" urged Jonathan. "Where were we — " He was interrupted by a burst of gunfire across the common. A group of minutemen dashed past the graveyard and crouched behind a house.

Ka-boom.

"Look at that smoke — what are they burning?" Matt pointed at three dark columns billowing toward the blue sky.

"They're burning houses, I bet." Emily was glad the Hartwells' house had escaped, but she wondered who lived in the ones going up in flames now.

"Anyway," said Jonathan pointedly, "we're looking for our connecting place. It's a simple matter" — his voice croaked, as if it might not be so simple — "of finding those headstones with enough space for three . . ."

There were several spots, Emily thought, that

looked sort of right. They started crawling among the headstones. Emily could feel an invisible line above her head, the line a cannonball would trace as it tore over the graveyard wall. Her breath got shorter, and it was hard to concentrate.

"Wait a minute, man," said Matt to Jonathan. "Didn't one of those headstones have the same first name as you? Jonathan somebody."

"Right," said Emily. The postcard picture popped into her head. "And the other guy's name — a weird one from the Bible."

"Hezekiah!" Jonathan, on his hands and knees, stiffened like a hunting dog. He pointed to the headstone in front of him.

"Yes," cried Emily. "And Jonathan Simonds, over there. Here we go." She scrambled toward the space between Jonathan Simonds and Hezekiah Smith.

When they had all crawled into their places, Matt and Emily looked at Jonathan. He held up the TASC control, then hesitated. "I hate to say this, but I think we have to stand up. Or it might not work right."

Jonathan didn't move, though. Neither did Matt or Emily.

Finally Matt said in a tight voice, "Okay, here goes. One, two, three — *up.*"

Emily rose with the others, feeling like a target. Jonathan held out the TASC control with a shaking hand. "Hold still for transport."

Then the weird tingling. Emily braced herself.

Ka-boom.

If you *were* hit by a cannonball, would it be the same coming-apart feeling as this? The same as disassembling your molecules to rush through time and space?

The next morning Emily slept so late that Mrs. Cowen checked to see if she was sick. "You didn't go to sleep that late last night," said Mrs. Cowen, feeling Emily's forehead. "You and Matt and Jonathan were going to bed when we got home."

Emily blinked up at her mother, trying to take in where she was — *when* she was. Then she sighed groggily. "I'm just tired. From softball, I guess."

Thankfully Emily remembered stuffing her Colonial costume under the bed before she fell asleep last night. She and Matt would have to do some secret laundry, especially Mom's shirts that the boys had borrowed. Or, wait — had the dirt from 1775 stayed there? In the confusion and hurry, she hadn't noticed.

"So, take your time getting up," Mrs. Cowen went on. "When you're ready, there's breakfast." She paused on her way out the door. "And after breakfast, *without fail,* you kids have to take that invention thing back to Grandpa Frank's."

"I know, we said we would." Emily crawled out of bed and pulled on jeans and a sweatshirt. She stuck a Band-Aid on her blistered heel. Coming out of the bathroom, she noticed the open door of Matt's room. Matt and Jonathan must be up already.

But there was the Time and Space Connector, an ungainly bulk in the middle of the room. Its projector still pointed at the blank wall, as if it were inviting Emily to choose a new destination.

"I can't," said Emily sadly. The three kids had agreed, before they went to 1775, that this would be their one last trip. They *had* to give the TASC back to Grandpa Frank today.

Following the smell of coffee and home fries, Emily found Matt and Jonathan and her mother at the kitchen table. Emily helped herself from the pans on the stove. She thought of her bowl of cornmeal mush in the Hartwells' dark, smoky kitchen. Here, sunshine fell across the vinyl floor. Mild air drifted through the large open windows.

Since Matt and Jonathan were sharing the comics from the Sunday paper, Emily picked up the sports page. But she found herself looking up at the boys as they silently ate and read. Just yesterday, the three of them had been together on an incredible adventure. They'd been an adventure team. Now that was all over. There wouldn't be any more adventures.

Mrs. Cowen folded her newspaper section and stood up. "I'm going out in the yard," she told the kids. "As soon as you finish eating, bring the thing down to the driveway, all right? We'll load it into the minivan."

In Matt's room a short while later, Emily watched her brother pin the posters back up in the blank space over his bed.

Matt, standing on his bed, glanced down at Emily. "What're you looking like that for? We were lucky to get to use the TASC one more time. We were lucky to ever get to use it in the first place."

"I know," said Emily heavily.

No one spoke for a moment. There were only ripping noises as Jonathan tore off long strips of package tape and fastened down loose parts of the TASC. Finally he looked up at Emily.

"Stop staring at me like that," Jonathan told her. "Did you already forget how we almost got killed back there? There ought to be a warning on this machine: 'History can be dangerous to your health.' "

"I know," said Emily. She felt as if nothing were ever going to be fun or exciting, ever again.

Matt and Jonathan wheeled the rattling TASC cart along the hall and carried it down the stairs. Emily went ahead, opening the front door for them.

In the driveway, Mrs. Cowen was waiting with the side door of the minivan slid open. The boys were lifting the TASC up when a blue rented car pulled into the driveway behind the van.

"I don't know why your father has to work on weekends," muttered Mrs. Cowen. But she hurried over to the driver's window. "Hi — you must be Mr. Kingsley from Pitcairn-Smith, Ltd., right? Dan's expecting you." She waved a hand at the open front door of the house. "But would you mind parking on the street? I was about to drive the kids across town to return — " She nodded toward the TASC as if she didn't know what to call it.

Mr. Kingsley backed his car out of the driveway, parked, and strolled over to the van. He peered at the TASC, which Jonathan and Matt were struggling to fit sideways through the van door. "This must be one of those famous Yankee inventions, eh?" He lifted the gray barbecue cover that hid the TASC. "What does this part do?" He poked at the clumps of batteries and instruments on the second shelf.

"Wouldn't touch that, if I were you," panted Jonathan. "Might get a — "

"Agh!" Mr. Kingsley jerked his hand back. "I got a shock! Dangerous, fooling around with a —"

"Time machine," Matt finished for him, grinning broadly.

Emily laughed in surprise. Mrs. Cowen laughed, too. "Oh, you've got to watch out with these time machines!"

Rubbing his shocked hand, Mr. Kingsley tried to smile. "A time machine! Have you taken any trips yet?"

"Yes, as a matter of fact," said Emily. For some reason, she was feeling a lot better. "We've just come back from the beginning of the American Revolution."

"Have you!" Mr. Kingsley gave her an uncle-ish smile. "And what did you learn from your little trip?"

Resting his hands on the TASC's gray cover, Matt gazed down from the van at Mr. Kingsley. In a deliberate tone he said, "We learned why the Americans *won* and the British *lost*."

Jonathan leaned out from the other side of the TASC. "See, the Americans were fighting to run their own lives. Fighting for their families and their farms and their villages."

Stepping up beside Matt and Jonathan, Emily turned to look the Britisher straight in the eye. "And the British just didn't get it."

Mrs. Cowen looked uneasy. Before Mr. Kingsley could answer, she broke in. "We shouldn't keep you chatting here, Mr. Kingsley — I know you and Dan have a lot of business to conduct." Waving him toward the house, she slid the van door shut on the three kids.

Riding in the joggling back of the minivan, Emily seemed to see the people she'd come across in 1775, in that most exciting moment in history. She saw Paul Revere, riding into Lexington on that moonlit road; the little Hartwell girls, waving good-bye to her from the cart; Abigail, with her innocent smile, pretending to help the British search. And Emily saw Ned, the British soldier who *did* get it, disappearing into the Colonial American landscape.

Jonathan, holding onto one leg of the TASC cart to keep it from rolling, cleared his throat. He'd been humming, the way he did when he was thinking hard. "Of course, some parts of history could be interesting, but not really that dangerous."

Matt had been staring toward the front of the van with a faraway expression. Now he glanced over the TASC at his friend. "Give it up, Schultz."

But Emily was sure that her brother had been

remembering, too. Remembering riding with Paul Revere, and listening to Captain Parker and his minutemen in Buckman's Tavern, and watching the Colonists chase the British across the Lexington common. And she had a feeling Matt was beginning to change his mind about never wanting to have any more adventures like that.

Emily leaned around the TASC to grin at Jonathan. "We'll give it up, right? Until next time."